THE HAND

THE HAND

A NOVEL | KOI SHIF

Deeds Publishing | Athens

Copyright © 2019—Koi Shif

ALL RIGHTS RESERVED—No part of this book may be reproduced in any form or by any electronic or mechanical means, including information storage and retrieval systems, without permission in writing from the author, except by a reviewer who may quote brief passages in a review.

This is a book of fiction based on true events. Names, characters, businesses, certain long-standing institutions, churches, agencies, places, events and incidents are either a product of the author's imagination or used in a fictitious manner.

Any resemblance to actual persons, living or dead, is purely coincidental. The names and identifying details have been changed to protect the privacy of individuals.

Published by Deeds Publishing in Athens, GA
www.deedspublishing.com

Printed in The United States of America

Cover design by Mark Babcock. Text layout by Matt King.

ISBN 978-1-947309-86-9

Books are available in quantity for promotional or premium use. For information, email info@deedspublishing.com.

First Edition, 2019

10 9 8 7 6 5 4 3 2 1

To my wife and two daughters. For showing me what the truth of love is. For endearing me with an unwarranted, never-ending stream of affection. For it is like the morning sun glistening off the wet dew on the reddest of roses and the most extravagant of lilies, and just when you do not think any more beauty could be revealed, without fail, on a new day, the sun rises again and shows the unlimited elegance it possesses. To my family, for exposing me to the most precious of unbridled love, I am eternally grateful.

PREFACE

The notion deep inside of me for these characters first came in the mid 90's. I was in my twenties and trudging my way through life. My late-night, pre-sleep thoughts would drift off into the possibilities of who they are, what they did, and what they might do.

It was not until the fall of 2018, after I had been living in Athens, Georgia for two years, that I had grown enough in this life to be open to the possibilities of what this universe has to offer and was ready to take action. It was then that I would put pen to paper and bring these characters to life within this book. For it is a story that I have put forth to share with you and I would be remiss if I did not recognize some of the great story tellers of all time that helped develop me in such a way that enabled this book to be written.

The stories of my youth were told to me through music. It was in my older brother's vinyl record collection that I was lucky enough to come across the likes of Bruce Springsteen and the E Street Band, Meatloaf and Jim Steinman, and of course, Pink Floyd with Roger Waters and David Gilmour. It was their mystical story telling that came from these vinyl platforms that opened my mind and led me to places yet unknown. The passion, the drama, the excitement, and the rock n' roll fantasies that drifted through my ears not only helped develop my creativity, but most certainly helped keep me here in this physical life.

I have stopped questioning the reasons why, in my younger, formative years, time and again I would rather have removed myself from this life rather than stay. For reasons only to be discovered much later in life, I was wrapped in the bondage of self, a bondage that caused me agony of the most unrelenting kind, an affliction that was embedded deep within me. It was as real to me as the ocean's tide and it was clear that these burdens were mine to bear.

But it was in those fantasies that Bruce, Meatloaf, Roger, and David sang about that I was able find solace from my wretched state. It was the singing of their tales, so eloquently intertwined with their music, that allowed me to escape to those places they so passionately led me to. Most of the time, I would rather go to those places of intrigue than stay where my two feet were planted.

Through Bruce's passion, I lived on the Backstreets and down Thunder Road. I would take frequent trips to Jungleland, and I would find shelter from my storm in the bellowing of Clarence's soul as it enveloped me with its warmth. Without a doubt, I always felt more comfortable where the darkness met the edge of town and knew with conviction that I despised the in-betweens. I was able to believe, even for the slightest moments of the day, that there was magic in the night.

There was power in the desperation and hope that rang

true and clear down to my bones when Meatloaf was Crying Out Loud. That chilly California breeze against our skin was worth dreaming of. I thought that if there was a heaven, it could wait.

As if Roger and David were speaking directly to me, knowing exactly how I felt, they eased my pain as I envisioned a distant ship and smoke on the horizon. Becoming entranced by Comfortably Numb and its transcendent guitar was good enough to get me through some of the times that seemed so horrible in my mind.

I would need to recognize my inspiration that's been drawn from Tom Clancy, J.K. Rowling, Stephen King, and Herman Hesse. Realizing that Tom really achieved success, in a very different career, at a much later stage in his life, has always stayed with me. Hearing that JK would patiently spend hours in cafés around England as her young daughter slept in the carriage beside her, plotting away with her stories, made me think well why not me? For Stephen, thinking the way he did and having enough willingness to share that with others. For Herman, helping me realize the importance of sitting and listening to the river in all its glory.

For my good friend's blind faith in giving me an opportunity, for his support, and for his generosity. If it were not for my good friend, I would not have been transformed by living in the Georgia woods for a year, a year that would continue my transition into the man I was always meant to be. A time of self-reflection accompanied only by the river, the sun, the moon, the stars, the trees, the flowers, and the animals. My time of solitude was all under the protective shroud of the deepest blue Georgia sky. A time and opportunity that only a rare few men would have in their lifetime.

For the uniqueness of standing up high on the green grassy knoll, with the early winter chill whisking against my face, as the morning light of the sun pierced through the leafless tree branches as it breached the crest of the formidable mountain, and with the morning silence transformed with the awakening of a new day, has been gifted within my soul, saving my life in every way possible.

For my friends unconditionally accepting me for who am I am. For letting me stand amongst them as complete uncertainty whirled throughout my life.

For Pat helping me realize that uncertainty is a virtue. For telling me that I should be open to what this universe has to offer, advice I can only repay by passing it along.

For Leo and the magic that is experienced when the paint is drying. The simplest of gestures changing my life and exposing me to Siddhartha and what the river is really about.

For our daily reprieve and the opportunity to live another day in this truly gifted life.

One

The midnight blues intertwined with the deepest of purples and some slivers of pinkish orange as they layered themselves across the horizon. An early evening showing of the fullest of grey moons has rested itself upon the colors of the night as it kept watch over us from the distance. The moon's reflection was elegantly shining off the waves as they crashed harmoniously on the white sand of the not so far-off beaches.

The wet steaminess of the Florida day had infiltrated the stadium. The now vacant rays of the sun had beat down relentlessly on the outer walls all day. The strength of the sun had baked the inside temperature and humidity to the most uncharacteristic and uncomfortable of conditions. No one inside could escape the dampness on their skin or the heat of the night.

The seatbacks throughout the stadium and dugouts are soaked from the sweat saturating through their shirts. On the commercial breaks, the production assistants are feverishly trying to dry the sweat from the TV personality's brow as they prepare to go back on the air.

"And, we are live in five-four-three-two-one…"

"This is Joe Coin joined by Marty Hightstown coming to you live, on a very warm and humid October night. There's an exhilarating atmosphere here at Tropicana Field in Tampa Bay, Florida. Well Marty, it should be an exciting game one of this World Series. We have these two pitching powers going head to head: the Tampa Bay Rays vs. the Chicago Cubs."

"Yes, this is very exciting, Joe! It is going to be a pitching duel in every game, especially tonight. And now that the Cubs have finally broken their curse by winning it all in 2016, we will have to see if the Rays are going to show up and stop them from earning another World Series Trophy. If the Rays bring their "A" game, it will be a very competitive series and the trophy could find its home here in Tampa Bay. It has been twelve long years since the Tampa Bay Rays have been to the championship series. It has been a long wait for the fans since their heartbreaking loss to Philadelphia in the 2008 series. Boy! What a great series that was. It was so competitive, but the Phillies were able to close it out in game five, not even needing to go the full seven games. Even though the Rays have been on this big stage before, they have yet to bring home the championship. Having home field advantage and having their fans behind them to start this series will give them an edge tonight. We will soon find out if this could be the year of the Rays!"

"Now Marty, we have to address this humidity and heat. I believe this is going to be the x-factor in tonight's game. Suddenly, these players must deal with a very unexpected situation. It is not the customary cool, fall October night that we usually have for the World Series. These guys will not be wearing any long sleeves to stay warm tonight."

"I definitely concur. Joe, this is on the borderline of being unbearable. Tampa Bay has a great indoor stadium that is usually air conditioned, so on a normal day the weather would not be a factor here in balmy Florida. But since about 7:30am, the stadium crew, Tampa Bay Electric, and the MLB have been working in a joint effort to bring the power back to the air conditioning system here in the stadium. Thankfully we have power for everything else: the lights, scoreboards, concessions, TVs, etc., are all working just fine. It is just the air conditioning system that has been down since probably sometime last night. It has become increasingly hot and humid in the stadium all day with no relief in sight."

"I agree with you. It will be another whole factor to deal with in game one of this series. Not only do the players need to deal with and control the excitement and nerves which game one of the World Series always brings, but now they will have this added factor of the heat and humidity. It will come down to which team has the better athletes that can rise to the occasion and which of the two managers have prepared their team, with very short notice, to play in these conditions."

"Don't kid yourself, Joe, the lack of air conditioning will certainly affect the players tonight. Both teams have had to change to lighter uniforms. We have noticed that they are hydrating more. The trainers have put out blocks of ice and cooling fans in each dugout, which you never see at a baseball game."

"I can't agree with you more, Marty. But just inclement weather has never entirely cancelled a World Series game in the past. We did have the earthquake of 1989 that postponed game three of that series in the Bay Area. And of course, the Series was postponed after the tragic terrorist attacks of September 11th, 2001. I am one hundred percent confident that these conditions will not cancel or delay this game of the 2020 World Series. We will certainly be playing ball tonight with these two baseball giants battling it out until we have a victor. Nothing is going to stand in our way."

"We will be back shortly after a word from our sponsors for the playing of the national anthem and the first pitch!"

* * *

"Welcome back to our TV audiences from around the world! Marty, I have to say this stadium is rocking! That was a powerful rendition of the national anthem."

"Hearing our national anthem always gives me chills. It is always a time of self-reflection for me which immediately gives me gratitude for living in this great country. It helps me be thankful for and remember the men and women of the armed forces that live and die every day for our freedom."

"To have the opportunity to enjoy sports in general and tonight we have the World Series. What a blessing. We sure are lucky."

"If they weren't already excited enough, the singing of the national anthem really got this capacity crowd going. It is intoxicating as all the Tampa Bay fans are standing on their feet and waving those dark blue towels. There are so many towels it looks like the ocean!"

"As the Rays take the field, the starting pitcher Fernando

Acebo takes the mound. The temperature is ninety-one degrees and the humidity is at eighty-eight percent. As the athletes stand in their dugouts, hanging over the railing, the sweat is dripping off their fingertips, drenching the golden-brown clay dirt of the baseball field. It seems as though Acebo just came out of the shower, for the perspiration is rapidly dripping from his nose, ears, and forearms."

"Joe, this is certainly going to make it interesting. It could be very difficult for Acebo to grip the ball as he would normally like to. Although watching him take his last few warmup pitches, it does not seem to be that much of a problem."

"Ok! Here we go for the first pitch of the World Series. Acebo is on the mound and Dave Stript is at the plate for the Cubs. Acebo takes his wind up and delivers an inside fastball for a called strike one. Wow! That was clocked at 99 miles per hour. Obviously, the heat and humidity did not affect Acebo on that first pitch. Here comes the second pitch. It looks like another fastball, and whoa! Stript took a swing and got all of that one!

"Going back, going way back in deep center field, to the warning track, it is going to be close. Going back is the center fielder Weaver. He is running in stride as he plants his right foot midway up the wall and reaches for the ball. The ball just whispers by the brown-leather tips of his glove."

"How great is that! A second pitch leadoff home run for Stript in game one of the World Series puts the Cubs up one zip. That certainly silenced this crowd. Look at these fans. That once frenzied sea of towels has now been replaced with that ever-so-common disgruntled look on the faces of the fans."

"Yes, Acebo is noticeably upset with himself. Obviously that one got away from him a little bit and Stript took full advantage of it. Stript loaded everything he had behind that one and sent it into the promised land. Acebo is taking a few minutes on the mound to regain his composure."

"Wait a minute. What is that? Is that blood on his shirt?"

"I am not sure what that is. That is certainly strange. Where is that coming from?"

"Now Suarez, the shortstop, has jogged over to the mound and is looking at the back of Acebo's shirt. They are both scratching their heads as they try to see where the blood is coming from. It just started to appear on the back and top of Acebo's shoulders while he was composing himself after that home run. With the humidity and heat, the back of his shirt has become saturated with what seems to be his own blood. The Rays' trainer and manager are now out at the mound trying to get to the bottom of this."

"Marty, we are trying to get a close enough view with our cameras, but I can't figure it out yet. Can you make out where the blood is coming from?"

"No, I can't. It does not seem as though Acebo is cut or injured in any way."

"Wait! Is that blood splatter on the pitching rubber? They all look down at the off white golden-brown dusted pitching rubber as it is accumulating spots of blood falling from somewhere. Where are those drops of blood coming from? Everyone is in a quandary out there. There it goes again, and the blood is clearly not coming from anyone standing on the mound."

Simultaneously, everyone looks up. Peering up at the center of the dome ceiling, straining their necks and eyes, they look at the small circular housing which contains multiple lighting fixtures. The housing is mounted right above the pitching mound. As the distant housing comes more into focus, it becomes evident that something is dripping from the center of that housing. It is increasingly dripping more blood, painting the once white rubber foot placement into a dirty, dark red blood color, which is now the pinnacle of the pitching mound for game one of the World Series.

"This is certainly out of the ordinary. Play has stopped and everyone in the entire stadium and the world-wide TV audience has devoted their attention to the center of the roof and that little housing that is located way above us, at the uppermost point of the dome. Can we try and get a close up and look to see if we can make heads or tails of what is going on?"

"Oh no! No! What the heck is that? That can't be. Is that a hand? Oh, my God, it is a hand."

A hand is hanging out from the center of the housing, covered in blood. The blood is profusely flowing from the fingertips down to the mound.

A dozen or so police officers are now seen frantically running up the catwalk leading to the entrance of the housing.

About five minutes of anxious uncertainty have passed. No answers are coming from anywhere as the screams from the stands echo in the stadium as the fans are realizing what they are looking at on the jumbo screen. Their once disgruntled faces from the first inning homerun have been replaced by the look of horror and disgust at the sight of the bloody hand. Finally, two plain clothed detectives are seen scaling up the catwalk. Their gold police shields are tethered on chains bouncing in unison with each step they take.

"Stop! Stop! Don't touch anything. Stop! Stop!"

The out of breath veteran detective, Gary Hurst, is heard yelling as he laboriously traverses the catwalk. Scurrying up twenty meters ahead is his new younger rookie homicide partner, Jake Blevins.

"Tell them, Jake. Tell them not to touch anything."

Jake reaches the small entrance to the housing, somewhat out of breath, but he is still standing upright. The physical climb to the top of the dome was not a problem. Jake is a young, good-looking man in his early thirties who keeps in good physical condition.

"STOP! DON'T MOVE!" Jake yells as he enters the housing, the twelve uniformed officers freeze in their tracks. "Has anyone touched anything?"

"No, not yet," replies one of the officers.

"I was the first one to enter the housing and I immediately checked for vitals on the victim. I did not detect a pulse or any breathing. I declared him dead at that moment. Other than that, I have not touched anything," states a second officer that is standing closest to the victim.

"Okay then. Everyone, very slowly, but surely retrace your steps back to this entrance. Without touching anything."

By this time, being very out of breath and profusely sweating, Gary finally arrives at the top of the catwalk, gasping for air as he bends over.

"Dddd, dddd, did you tell them Jake?"

"Yes, Gary. No one touched anything. And I got them all out of the housing."

"Good. Call in the forensics team. Get them here ASAP."

"Jake, what about the victim?"

"When I entered the housing, the officer that was first on the scene informed me that he had immediately checked for vitals on the victim. The victim was not breathing, and the officer could not find a pulse. He died before any of the officers entered the housing."

Gary looks at the freshly inflicted, large wound, on the side of the victim's neck which is slowly oozing blood. "Considering the size of that neck wound and the amount of blood loss, it would have been a miracle if he was still breathing and had a pulse."

"I want all these unis off this platform and back down the catwalk. We need forensics to go over not only this room but also the entire catwalk with a fine-toothed comb."

The uniformed officers start making the long walk down the catwalk. "And don't touch anything," yells Hurst.

* * *

The figures in the dimly lit, dust covered, office-like room slowly come to focus. They're wearing gloves, booties, and hair nets. Their t-shirts are soaked with sweat because of the humidity. With the word FORENSICS clearly emblazoned across the back, the team meticulously and patiently scours the room for clues.

They scan the crime scene, the centerpiece of which is a clearly staged, dead body. The victim is in an upside-down vertical position. He is duct taped to the front side of a large filing cabinet. The victim and the cabinet are located near a two-foot by two-foot opening in the floor. His arm and part of his shoulder are dangling through the hole. The victim's hanging right arm is secured to his head with duct tape. This makes his arm and hand point in the downward position out of the hole and down to the field. He is tightly secured with the duct tape, so tightly that his back is flat against the metal file cabinet without a slouch. The soles of his sneakered feet are near the top edge of the cabinet. This position exposes his front side as he is facing outward.

Even though his head is secured to his arm, it is slightly turned and immobilized to his left. Being in this position, the right side of his neck is exposed where there is a very large bloody wound. The upside-down victim is wearing jeans and a Chicago Cubs t-shirt, all of which seem brand new. The position of the victim places him directly above the pitcher's mound.

The victim's right carotid artery has been violently punctured, making for a gaping exit path for the river of blood to flow freely. The blood rushed down his arm as if it were desperately trying to get somewhere. It flowed down his right shoulder, bicep, and forearm to ultimately engulf his hand. It found a way to ooze off his fingertips and find its way down onto the pitcher's mound. Although the blood had to travel a long distance, the lack of air flow in the stadium made for an uninterrupted journey. Because the air conditioning system was shut down, there was zero air movement in the stadium, so the drops of blood easily found their way directly to the mound below.

The hand was configured in such a way that the pinky, ring, and middle fingers were curled inward toward the palm, leaving the index finger and thumb to dangle at will, but rather straight. The tips of his pinky, ring, and middle fingers were epoxied together and to his palm so that they stayed in that fixed position.

Detective Jake crouched in the background studying the corpse. Still sweating, Gary has finally regained his composure from his labored breathing and now takes in air with some ease. Some time passes as he starts to analyze the scene in his head.

"What a sick psycho!" Jake says softly. "What do you think, Gary?"

There is no reply as Gary slowly turns his head, leading his worn, dark brown eyes to gaze at the body and the crime scene.

So, this is it. Gary thinks to himself. *This is a sort of game to this killer. After thirty plus years as a profiler, and the chief of the Chicago homicide unit, this is the game that will read as my final chapter.*

Obviously, our killer wanted to make a big statement. He wanted to put on a show on a big stage. He intentionally has started it this way. He has a vision. He has a mission and a plan that needs to be accomplished. He is smart and does not think he makes any mistakes. There is definitely a reason behind this. He has motivation. Something stimulated this sick bastard to start this game and to make this kill. He has planned and put too much thought into what he does. Which tells me he likes it, he likes the challenge, and he hates to lose. He has a yearning deep within his soul that has to be fed. He is not going to stop on his own. We will need to find out the root of that gaping hole deep down inside him, the hole that he is so desperately trying to fill. Getting a glimpse into that desire, into that need, into the reason behind what created this sick man, that will be the way we can catch him.

It is going to be very difficult to catch this one. But as we sit trying to figure this out today, he has already moved on. He's well into the selection of his next victim, well into the planning of his next kill. Planning the big stage that this story of his will continue to play out on.

He is probably damaged goods, stemming from something in his past. But what?

Whatever it was, he has overcome it for the most part. This and future killings are victories for him. They represent success for him. He's trying to show his ability to overcome whatever had happened that ultimately created him.

He is probably in his mid to late 30's, physically fit and strong. Somehow, he is very strong. He had to physically get this victim all the way up here, and duct tape him upside down to the file cabinet. He has above average intelligence and is extremely patient and poised.

"Gary, are you with us? Gary … Gary what are your thoughts?" The police are only about halfway through taking head shots, gathering pictures with their smart phones as they try to document and identify every facility worker that would have had access to the crime scene.

Gary finally speaks. "Really no need for that. It is probably a waste of time, but they can finish that task if it is going to help us appease the public outcry. Our guy, and yes, I believe this killer is a guy, is long gone, not even in close proximity to the stadium anymore. Wherever he is, he is probably in complete bliss and euphoria. Knowing that this story has started, the story he has created, and that it's being played on his terms for the whole world to witness. He is well in the lead, the advantage is his, and he is relishing his first victory.

"Get a team to start gathering all the CCTV videos from the stadium and parking lots and bring them to the local station. We are going to be here in Tampa for a while. At least until we get a grasp on what is going on. So you better call that lady friend of yours and tell her we won't be back to Chicago anytime soon."

"Well…hell of a first case to be working together!" Jake exclaims.

Alan Crate, the chief medical examiner, has been meticulously combing the body and the 15 feet around the victim. His team has been detailing and taking pictures of the rest of the room and are starting to make their way down the catwalk, metal step by metal step, gathering all fingerprints, any hair follicles or anything that might give them some DNA.

"Alan, any thoughts? Do we have a time of death?"

"Nothing yet. This guy is seemingly pretty good. We have not found a trace of anything yet but give us some time, Gary. We will find you a way in. We will get something. As far as the time of death, to get a precise time, with this heat and the humidity, that is going to be very difficult. But considering the current and almost normal body temperature of the victim right now, combined with our witnessing of the extreme blood flow that occurred down to the pitcher's mound, I will put the time of death within the last hour. This guy probably took his last breath shortly before the first officers arrived on the scene."

"Jake, that puts us right around the time of the national anthem. That puts the killer still up here right up until the start of the game. Have a focus of sixty minutes prior and after the national anthem as a timeline and focal point for reviewing all the CCTV footage. Maybe we can catch something as he left. He must have been up here most of the day. The distraction of power outage that took out the air conditioning system most likely helped him gain cover, making it easier for him to slip through security and work around the edges where no one was going to notice him.

"If I am to venture a guess, he probably made his exit when the lights were dimmed for the singing of the national anthem, which was then followed by total darkness as the fireworks exploded over the outfield stands. The entire stadium and live TV coverage were focused on that five-minute fireworks display. When the lights were out, that is when this guy, probably confidently, with a swagger that only a triumphant man would have, so calmly walked down the catwalk and made his way to an exit. With the lights coming on, the stadium was still filled with smoke from the fireworks, which continued to cause even more of a distraction."

Two

A few very bright lights illuminate an otherwise dimly lit room. The radiance is shining down on the now naked body of the victim. The body is laying backside down on a very cold metallic slab, part of the examination table where the victim lies in wait for his autopsy. Chief Medical Examiner Alan is dressed in scrubs from head to toe with his round, black-framed glasses laying gently across the bridge of his nose. He is peering into the very large wound in the victim's neck.

Gary and Jake enter the room. Gary states he wants limited access to this John Doe and all the evidence that has been gathered. He doesn't want a shred of tampering or a single careless mistake to jeopardize the investigation.

"What do you have for us, Alan?"

Alan slowly raises from the bent over position and starts to vocalize his thoughts. "The entry wound into the neck is quite large and deep. Twelve inches deep to be exact. The entry point being on the right side of the neck and, whatever the weapon, it was driven right through his carotid artery. And in this case, because the body was situated upside down, the weapon was thrust upward through his neck and through the center of his chest cavity. It pierced the right side of his heart, extending through the superior vena cava and the right atrium. The final resting point of the weapon was right in the middle of the right ventricle. The entry wound is two inches wide, and strangely enough is seemingly octagonally shaped. There is only one, direct, clear entry wound, meaning the weapon was just inserted one time and swiftly withdrawn from the victim, making for a very clean and direct pathway from the heart to the point of entry, creating a precise tunnel for the blood to flow out of the body.

"The bruising and pooling of his internal blood, due to the tightness of the duct tape used to secure him, gives us an estimated timeline of how long he was in that position. I estimate between ten and sixteen hours. That means he was secured upside down to the file cabinet anywhere between three A.M. and nine A.M. on the day of the murder.

"Other than the bruising and the entry wound, there are no other signs of trauma to the body. The cause of death was not the stabbing, but exsanguination, the massive blood loss as a result of the stab wound—meaning this John Doe was still alive as he bled out onto the pitcher's mound.

"Another most intriguing find is the purposeful configuration of the right hand. The killer used epoxy to curl and attach the ends of his pinky, ring, and middle finger to the palm of his hand. The killer left his other two digits alone, allowing his index finger and thumb to dangle and hang at their own will. These two fingers followed a relatively straight line pointing outward.

"We have not found any other trace amounts of fiber, DNA, or fingerprints on this body. We did find a large amount of some type of opiates in his system, probably oxycontin which were taken through the pill form. We did not find any track marks on the body, but we did find impression marks on the sublingual papilla, which is the bottom side of the mouth, underneath the tongue. The oxycontin pills were probably placed there for a rapid delivery method through the lingual veins, which leads right to the internal jugular vein. John Doe was very subdued, but still aware of his surroundings. He did not have the ability to respond or react to outside stimuli because of the large amounts of opiates running through his system. His sedation, most likely, enabled the killer to transport him to the scene of death and position him upside down without much fight or any resistance on his part."

"What about the room that the body was found in?" Gary asks.

"Don't know much about it or why it was set up with a desk, chair and filing cabinet. It was so dusty it obviously had not been used in years. The filing cabinet was moved eight feet from the side wall to the center of the housing to place him right next to the opening in the floor where our John Doe was found. The opening in the floor was previously used to access and maintain the lighting underneath the housing.

"We collected only three sets of prints from inside the housing and we are running those through the database as we speak. We also found a ten and a half size, right foot running sneaker shoe print in the dust. Just the right foot and only one print at that. No other prints and nothing regarding the left foot. We are also running the multitude of fingerprints that were lifted from the catwalk handrails.

"Other than that, Gary, this is all we have as of now. I promise we will work day and night with you to catch this guy. He is one deranged and twisted individual."

"Jake, what did the unis find out about our John Doe?"

"We do not have a positive ID yet. It has not even been twenty-four hours yet, but we are still running his fingerprints through the database. We are also using his photo trying to get a hit in the facial recognition database. But we still do not have anything. I think it is still too early to start putting his photo out to the media to try and ID him."

"Ok, I agree. Keep running those prints. We must find out who this John Doe is. Let's get back upstairs to the offices. The FBI, the Governor of Florida, and the Tampa Bay chief of police have all given me the go ahead to lead this investigation. We are going to be based out of these offices for now.

"First things first. Start setting up our photo board of evidence, check in to find out where we are with the CCTV footage, and if we have had any hits on the three fingerprints found at the crime scene. But, before any of that, get with the Tampa Bay Rays' owner and find out who used to work in that office perched high above the center of his stadium."

Three

Having finally changed out of the Chicago Cubs jersey that he was wearing for the World Series Game, Gary is suited up in his usual professional detective attire. He's outfitted in his pressed slacks, starched blue shirt, and a dark red tie which neatly brings him all together. His tie is lightly loosened a few inches and his top button is undone. He's deep in thought, standing in front of four large working white pin boards. The photos of the John Doe and the crime scene are attached to one of the boards. The remaining three boards are still empty. He gazes at the pictures as the once hot black coffee in the paper cup he holds turns to lukewarm at best.

Tapping his foot as he stares at the photos of the crime scene, the still unidentified first victim, only referred to as John Doe number one, stares blankly back at Gary. The victim's fingerprints are yet to get a match in any database so far. Gary's eyes draw closer to the picture of the hand that dripped the blood and he wonders, *what is the significance of the thumb and index finger staying straight while the pinky, ring, and middle are curled inward and epoxied to the palm to make the formation? Yes, maybe it makes for a good pathway for the blood to drip from his index finger. But I think this would be too much of an obvious intention. It means something more, much, much more. Why did the killer do that?*

Jake walks through the door into the large office space, having changed clothes himself. He is looking young, sharp, and vibrant, minus the tie.

"Gary, I found out more about the housing where the victim was found. It was an office used to support and maintain the lighting that comes from the center of the dome. It was used as a small office, occupied by Terry Schyminski up until about two years ago. For the fifteen years prior, Terry had to constantly change those light bulbs and maintain the systems. This was an important job, for that is a critical area for lighting in the stadium. Now for the interesting part. Two years ago, Terry was let go because they upgraded the entire lighting system for the stadium, implementing LED lighting which is now completely run from computers. So, the need for manual human maintenance was no longer required.

"Terry is a forty-seven-year-old decorated special operations veteran with twenty-six confirmed military kills. He had been working at the stadium since he got out of the military. Apparently, he loves the game of baseball. After speaking with the Tampa Bay Rays front office, it seems that Terry was very disgruntled when they had to let him go. Upon his departure, he did not do anything major. The witness said he only gave some verbal threats on the way out.

"One of the three sets of fingerprints found in the housing

belonged to Terry. Out of the three sets, the majority of the fingerprints were Terry's. The second pair of prints belonged to a stadium worker who passed away eighteen months ago from natural causes. The third set of prints, which were only two partials, a thumb and index finger, from seemingly the same hand, have yet to be identified."

"Do we have a whereabouts on Terry?"

"We have a last known address of 22 Wakefield Place. That's right here in Tampa, about eight miles from the stadium."

"Ok, that is a good enough connection for me. I have a hunch on this guy. Let's go see if we can pay Terry a little visit."

FBI Agent Christine and FBI Agent Ryan are two young local bureau agents stationed in Tampa Bay. They were assigned to Gary's team to work this case. They are sitting at the two other desks in the large office.

"Christine and Ryan! Come with us as we check into this Terry guy."

With blues skies overhead and barely a cloud in sight, the team of four exit the station and walk across the parking lot. It is midday on this hot humid Florida afternoon as the detectives and agents make their way to their two very plain, unmarked police cars.

Gary starts giving direction as they walk. "We are only going to talk to him. We want a silent approach. No sirens and no lights. We do not want to alarm him. Jake and I will go and knock on the front door. Christine and Ryan, you both hang back about 30 feet."

The two grey police cars park right outside a slightly below average looking two-bedroom house. The grass is land-scaped, but looks as though it has not been attended to in a bit. As they approach the house, making their way up from the cracked sidewalk to the walkway, Gary gives a motion to have the two agents wait right there, at the beginning of the walkway. Gary and Jake start their walk towards the house. Perspiration noticeably drenches their shirts as they study the drawn shades that are covering all the windows.

The sound of a window breaking comes from the front of the house. As the detectives crouch a bit, but do not run, a voice beckons, "I didn't do it! It wasn't me!"

"We just want to talk, Terry, that's all, just talk. Why don't you let us in?" Two high- powered rifle shots ring out from the direction of the broken window, hitting the dirt and walkway next to Gary and Jake. All four cops run for cover.

"I said I didn't do it! This is my house! Get off my property! I'm not bothering anyone and I don't want to talk. Go away!"

Jake dives over the hood of the car as Gary runs skidding around the back bumper. They join Christine and Ryan who are already behind the car.

"Anyone hit?"

"No, I'm good."

"No not here, but man that was close."

"Just a hunch huh! Maybe we are on to something here."

Jake slowly opens the back door to his squad car and re-trieves a rifle with a scope. He perches himself on the opened car door. He has a direct line of sight to the window where the shots came from.

"Do you see anything?"

"No. No movement, nothing."

"Terry, my name is detective Gary Hurst working with the Tampa PD. I believe you did not do it. I just want to talk … man to man." There is no response.

With a quieter voice, Gary turns one eye to Jake.

"Just keep a sharp eye on him. I do not want you shooting at him. We want him alive. Also, this guy is decorated specials ops military. If he wanted us dead, those two shots would have been directly through our hearts. I think he is scared. He must have seen it on TV and put two and two together. He suspected we'd be coming and he has prepared himself."

A very loud and emotional voice started screaming from the house as Terry finally responded. "I don't want to talk, I just want to be left alone. I don't bother anyone; I served my country with honor and served the Tampa Bay Rays with honor as well for fifteen years. What do I get in return? I lose my job. I am replaced by a computer! Now I am just living on welfare and military retirement which does not add up to much. This is all very disrespectful for someone who served their country. I made this country a safer place to live for people like you."

"What do you see, Jake?"

"I can see his outline. I have a clear shot if needed. He has a rifle which is aimed right at us. I can see between the curtains. He has a large arsenal of guns and ammo stacked behind him. I do not think he is coming out of there without a fight."

"I saw that guy on the television! I saw his arm hanging out of what used to be my old office way up above the field. I did not kill that guy. I killed many an enemy in the service, but I did not kill that guy. I have not even been back to the stadium since they let me go. It was not me. Now would you just leave?"

By this time, twenty plus black and whites, with sirens blaring and cherry tops flashing, had stationed themselves up the street. All the local unis had their guns drawn, all pointed at Terry. Two black armored SWAT Humvees pulled up directly behind the two unmarked cars parked in front of the house. The tactical team barreled out the back with helmets on and guns drawn, ready for action. The parking of the two oversized vehicles nose to nose created a safe zone on the far side of the trucks for a command center to take hold. The Tampa Bay Police Chief Smith and the overzealous mayor, Jimmy Sphynxter, who is currently campaigning for his run to be the governor of Florida, were riding in the second vehicle and are now standing in the command center with the SWAT Team leader.

From the safety of the command center, the Tampa Bay Police Chief Smith beckons Gary to join them behind the trucks for an assessment of the situation. "I am a bit busy right now!" Gary yelled back.

"Gary! This is Mayor Sphynxter. We need you to join us back here immediately! I command you to fall back and join us." With impatience obvious in his un-authoritative voice, the mayor exclaimed his wishes.

Knowing he did not have time for this type of egotistical pissing match right now and against his better judgement, Gary tells Jake not to take his scope off of Terry and that he will be right back. Gary briefly leaves his team and falls back to converse with the higher ups.

"What do we have here? Is this our guy?" Sphynxter asks,

with his unusually high and squealy voice that still has hints of a New York accent.

"I'm not sure yet. He may be, but he may not be."

Surprisingly, Sphynxter replies, "We are instructing SWAT to take over. This is obviously our guy. His prints were all over the crime scene. He already has taken two shots at you guys. We need to stop this guy before he kills someone else. The Tampa Bay community is scared enough. We have a killer on our hands. We need to give them something so they feel at ease again, so they go back out and start spending their money again! I command you and your team to step down, Detective Gary Hurst."

"Mayor! I have been put in charge in this investigation. I have the blessing of the FBI, the current governor of Florida, and the President of the United States."

With a very sarcastic tone, Sphynxter replied, "Well sorry. We are in the midst of an active shooter in the territory, that as acting mayor, I oversee. There is no question about who has authority here. I am taking over. Chief Smith, order your SWAT team to take their positions and prepare for entry to take this guy down."

Chief Smith does not respond and looks at both Sphynxter and Hurst.

"Mayor, we need to take a minute and assess the situation." Chief Smith is obviously in support of Detective Gary.

"If you like having the Chief in front of your name you best get your men in place."

"Yes, mayor."

As the Chief radios his team to take their positions, Gary states his case.

"This might not even be our guy! We need him alive. He's not going anywhere, let's take some time to do this right."

"Your input is heard. Now stand down, Detective Gary."

Shouts from the house are heard. "Gary…are you still out there?"

"Yes, I am still here, Terry."

"I see the SWAT team and the police cars. You better tell them to back off, I am not kidding."

"Ok, ok, I will."

The SWAT team members continue to scurry to their positions.

"I see them moving. Order them down. I know what they are doing, I have military training. I know what they are doing."

"Mayor, I beg of you. Let me just try and talk him out. You can take all the credit. We will make it your day. Think of what this will do for your campaign if we catch this guy alive."

The mayor ponders. "OK, I'll give you a chance."

"Good, good."

Gary quickly joins his team again behind the two grey cars directly in front of the house. "Okay team, we don't have much time if we're going to bring this guy out alive. Stay alert and follow my lead." Gary stands up and puts his hands up in a surrendering motion and yells out to Terry.

"Look, I'm putting my gun down."

Without taking his eye out of his scope and having his gun locked directly on the shadowy figure behind the curtains, Jake whispers "Are you sure, Gary?"

"It's our only chance, I have to get him to trust me and to

understand that we are not going to hurt him. Nobody shoot, nobody."

Gary steps out from behind the car with his hands raised and slowly starts walking towards the house.

"I come in peace, Terry."

"It doesn't look like it. I said you better tell your teams to back down!"

"They are under orders not to shoot. We just need to talk our way through this and everything will be okay."

In the meantime, the mayor has gotten with the captain of the SWAT team; he orders that on his command, the team is to hit that house with a dozen flash grenades and make an entry to apprehend this guy.

Gary is now halfway up the walkway and is engaging with Terry as he walks.

"Okay, that's close enough. We can talk fine with you right there."

"I just want to get a bit closer. It'll be more productive if we do not have to yell every word." For the first time since his initial shots out of the window, Terry place his rifle on the window ledge and takes a bead on Gary, but does not engage.

The mayor, trying to be authoritative in his high squealy voice, yells out, "Go, go, go," as he nervously tries to give his command to the SWAT team captain. Loud bursts are heard exploding from the grenade launchers as they hurl the flash bombs through the windows and into the house. As Terry retreats into his house, he slips backward and accidently discharges multiple shots from his rifle straight up into the ceiling. The SWAT team immediately returns fire.

Gary hits the ground and covers his head shouting, "NO, NO, NO!"

Terry takes cover in a back room.

Within seconds after the three-minute barrage of bullets that just destroyed the front of the small two-bedroom house, the dozen SWAT team members, dressed in black with Kevlar, smoke masks, and helmets, aggressively kick through what is left of the front and back doors. Methodically clearing each room as they go, they do not encounter any return fire or engagement from Terry. As two of the SWAT team members enter the back room, they find Terry in a sitting position against the back wall, slouched over to the left a bit, with his rifle still propped up under his chin, his finger still on the trigger, and his head blown out his back side. The innards of his skull are painted all over the mustard yellow wall behind him.

Gary, now up and running to the front door, is followed closely by Jake and his two other agents. He enters the house, making his way to the back room and sees the dead body. In disgust and frustration, he looks up and screams, "DAMMIT!"

The afternoon had darkened from the daily visit of afternoon thunderstorms which are so common in Florida. A very smug Mayor Sphynxter, with an unearned confidence and cockiness, addresses the TV cameras and news reporters in front of the yellow police tape that is strewn about 50 yards in front of the small house that up until about three hours ago very happily housed Terry Schyminski.

Sphynxter smiles into the cameras as he says, "The residents of the Tampa Bay community can now rest at ease. Under my direction, we have put an end to the terror that has plagued this city for the days since the murderous act that was committed during game one of the World Series. It is time for our community and baseball fans from all over to come back and start enjoying everything Tampa Bay has to offer. It is time to go back out and start spending money in this great city. It is time to play ball. Let this great city get on with hosting the World Series. And, yes, of course, GO RAYS!"

* * *

Chief Medical Examiner Allan is hovering over the dead body. "No real mystery here. Cause of death is a self-inflicted gunshot wound. Point of entry is under the chin and exiting right out the crown of the skull."

The rest of the forensics team is dusting for prints in the almost destroyed house. Jake is intently looking over the arsenal of guns, ammo, and the collection of about fifty knives. The knives range from a two-inch pocket Boy Scout knife to special ops military grade blades to one actual samurai sword.

"We need to get all these back to the station and start examining them for any clues that might match the murder weapon from our John Doe number one. I want them all dusted and tested for DNA to see if there is a match."

Medical Examiner Allan replied, "Yes Jake, I agree. There is no duct tape anywhere to be found. There is nothing else that might have helped Terry execute that killing at the stadium. Look at all his shoes. They are size nine. Terry had very small feet. The footprint at the stadium was a size ten and a half from a running sneaker. These are mostly combat boots."

Gary joins the conversation. "I agree, check all the knives. I think the only thing accomplished today was the unfortunate death of a decorated veteran. Although his death will be ruled a suicide, the blood on that yellow wall is really on the hands of our misguided Mayor Sphynxter."

Four

Weeks had passed since the failed attempt at apprehending Terry Schyminski. Despite the lack of evidence connecting him to the murder, the mayor was still sticking to his story that the killer had been disposed of. Even though Sphynxter had been reprimanded by the President of the United States, the FBI Director, and the current Governor of Florida, he was still hitting the gubernatorial campaign trail hard. While there was an ongoing investigation into his unauthorized leadership and command at the Terry Schyminski raid, he no longer had any oversight with the police force or Chief Smith. The FBI had made it clear that Detective Gary Hurst and his team would lead this investigation and had the full resources of the FBI and US Government at his disposal.

After examining the entire collection of knives and blades from Schyminski's house, there was no DNA or possible match for any murder weapon that would link Terry to the killing.

Standing in the center of the investigation room, with the crime scene photos taking up two of the four whiteboards in the background, Gary was speaking with his team of Jake, Christine, and Ryan. He posed some unanswered questions.

"How do we not have an ID on our John Doe? It has been weeks. We need to try more databases. How has this guy gone undetected? What about the two other partial prints that we found at the scene as well? How do we not have any connections, matches or leads to go on? Jake, what is it that we do have? Give us an update."

Jake replied, "The duct tape is your basic run of the mill duct tape that can be purchased at any hardware store, general market, or shopping mall for that matter. The killer is good. He must have been wearing gloves the entire time. We have not found any DNA other than the victim's on the many rolls of duct tape that were used to secure him to the file cabinet. The ten and a half running shoe is a Nike. But there is nothing unique about a size ten and a half men's running shoe from Nike. It can be purchased online or just about anywhere in the world. All we have to go on with the shoe is the size.

"We have had the FBI Information Technology team looking deep into the situation with the CCTV camera footage that we retrieved from the stadium."

"How is there nothing on those?" Gary asked.

"Well it's just that. There's nothing. Nothing viewable on those from anywhere in the stadium or the surrounding parking lots. It only shows blue screen. All the cameras in the stadium and the parking lots are overseen by the Tampa Bay Rays organization and there is nothing to show.

"Our suspect is extremely smart and has a very high IQ. He is probably also well educated. I would say at least four years, if not more, in a very high academic institution. The entire CCTV system is digitally based on a hard drive. This system records everything to a central hard drive system. This system was hacked, presumably by our killer, and all that was recorded for the three days before Game One of the World Series was a blue screen. The FBI thinks the footage is somewhere, they just have not located it yet. They have their best people working on it. They haven't been able to infiltrate into the program that is hiding the footage or find out where the footage is being hidden."

"Why didn't any of the security officers notice the blue screen? We were leading up to the World Series for crying out loud."

"That is also an interesting thing. The killer looped a digital recording of the days leading up to one of the divisional championship games, making the footage appear to be live. Even though they were just watching a previously recorded loop, they still believe the live footage was being recorded elsewhere. Our guy is probably one of the best computer hackers in the world. Educated at the highest level. He also hacked the computer system that controlled the air conditioning for the entire stadium. That is how he controlled the power outage that took down all the air systems on game day."

"Unbelievable! I am intrigued with how this suspect's mind works! This guy has really thought things out. He is very well organized and plans for everything. Well, with this level of intelligence, he must have been trained somewhere? Start looking into what institutions teach IT at this level. There must be a record of him somewhere. He must have made an impression on a teacher or mentor somewhere along the line. Also, reach out into the entire IT department for the FBI and CIA. They are the best we have and may have crossed paths with our suspect in the past. Also start interviewing any high-end hackers that have been incarcerated. Someone must have run across our guy at some point."

* * *

As night fell, Gary and Jake watched the news on a TV hanging above the bar they were sitting at. On the screen the mayor was campaigning. Their plates were empty of the burgers they just ate, with only remnants of ketchup and a few French fries remaining. With their sleeves rolled up to their elbows, they were leaning on the bar. Jake took a swig of his half full mug of beer. The tired detectives were at a loss, barely having a glimmer of hope for finding a lead to the killer who terrorized the world as baseball fans from all over sat and watched the top of the first inning in game one of the World Series.

Gary, barely awake, began to speak. "We will get him, we always do. It doesn't seem like it now, but we will. We will get a hit. Someone saw something. Saw this or saw that. And those prints...we will get a match on those prints." As Gary came to life a little bit more, his eyes started to widen. "Our guy is not done, not nearly done. He made a statement at that game. He wants everyone to watch, he wants to be noticed as if he has a message to send. He is meticulous in his planning and I believe he has a very long, drawn out plan waiting to be delivered. He wants to play with us for as long as he can. Jake, this has only just begun. I hope you are ready to do whatever it takes to get this guy with me."

Jake, on the edge of sleep, was still slouching. His hand was holding up his chin, supported only by his elbow on the bar. "Absolutely! I am all in Gary," Jake said without opening his eyes. "We are going to get this guy if it is the last thing we do. I just need a little shut eye right now."

Five

As the mid-morning sun illuminated the investigation room, penetrating the windows from the east, to the west there was a distant sight of the Gulf's grey blue water sparkling the rays like a mirror. Agents Christine and Ryan quietly sat at their desks perusing crime scene notes while detective Gary stood intently in front of the chronological photo board. Jake's desk was only attended by his empty chair and a cold cup of coffee that was the culprit responsible for the stains on the various notes scattered across his desk.

Christine and Ryan were thumbing through all the interviews of the facility workers at the stadium that may have seen something out of the ordinary in the days leading up to game one of the World Series.

As he stares at the photos in front him, Gary's mind is deep at work, desperately trying to coax himself into thinking like their suspect—trying to find answers to the many questions poised in front of him. He longs to understand the motivation driving their killer. He knows they are behind the eight ball and are quite challenged with their progress of the investigation, not having as much as a lead to pursue. He persistently starts asking himself questions. The self-inquiry and debate are whirling around in his mind.

What is making this killer tick? What created the need for him to put on such a display in front of the whole world? Why was this particular individual chosen? Why game one of the World Series? Why place the victim in such a way that the blood would drain out? What was used as a murder weapon? Obviously, something unique was used, but what? How did he apprehend the victim and why hasn't anyone reported someone missing yet?

What about the significance of the hand? Why display only the hand and part of the arm as it dangled out of the housing far above the pitcher's mound? He probably could have hung most of the body out of that opening, which would have had more of an impact, but he purposely just made the hand visible. Why did he purposefully epoxy the ends of those three fingers to his palm, but not the index nor the thumb. Having it in that formation is telling us something. Something that has to do with his motivation, but what?

How long has he been planning this? Probably a long time. One can't put a spectacle like this on overnight.

Jake comes walking through the clear glass double doors leading to the large space that sufficed for an investigation room. His button-down shirt is half untucked from his jeans, visibly showing his brown leather belt with its bronze buckle in front. He grabs for his cold black coffee that had been sitting on his desk for hours. "Gary get this, I have been up all night studying these photos. All the photos from the crime scene. My focus kept leading back to these two blown up pictures of the partial prints, the ones found on the corner of the file cabinet that our John Doe was duct taped to. One of a thumb and one of an index finger. I noticed how in both partial prints, the edges are straight lines. And because of the lack of DNA found at the scene, we all think the killer is wearing some type of glove. Right?

Gary is now facing Jake. He's intrigued. He nods his head in agreement as he follows Jake's logic.

"I think he messed up. I think his gloves got ripped. Or maybe they were possibly sliced open by something. Maybe he cut it on the sharp edge of the metallic file cabinet as he was moving it to the edge of the opening in the floor, resulting in the two, small straight edged slits in the gloves, exposing him for these partial prints to be left on the cabinet."

"Yes, possibly. I like where you are going with this, Jake. If they were surgical type gloves, they could be easily be cut open by the sharp edge of the metallic cabinet. But why didn't we find any more prints to match these two? If his fingers were exposed, he must have touched something else?"

"I don't know yet. Maybe he realized the two small slits were there and replaced the gloves with another set."

"Yes, that could be. So why is it that we have we not had a hit on these prints yet? Could it be that our suspect has never done anything in his whole life that warranted a fingerprint?"

"I've been asking myself the same question all night. I thought we must not be running it through the correct database. We have the local Florida database, the FBI national database, the CIA terrorist database all coming up negative. There are at least three other databases that I could think of that we haven't tried yet.

"We think our guy is very strong, having transported this victim from who knows where all the way to the heights of the Tampa Bay Rays domed stadium. This is no small task. It would take some brute strength and a certain fitness level to accomplish such a feat. I think maybe this guy is an athlete or was an athlete. The NCAA and United States Olympic Committee both have databases on all their athletes. These databases contain bios, social security numbers, and yes, fingerprints. They were primarily used in getting the teams clearance to travel through the airports, and the bios were used for media releases. There would be no reason for these to be crossed with the FBI, CIA, or local law enforcement's databases that we have been searching. I reached out at three in the morning to our FBI counterparts and they were contacting the NCAA and the USOC first thing this morning to gain access to their databases.

"You mentioned three databases. The NCAA and the USOC are only two."

"I would not give much credence to my third idea. Like you, Gary, I was raised Catholic. I was very strongly considering entering the priesthood for the Catholic church. I even took a semester at seminary school to look into the process. As it turned out, my true calling was to law enforcement and serving my community in that capacity.

"But I remembered some things from my one semester at

seminary school. They had a class on teaching the process for becoming a Catholic priest. The Catholic church is one of the oldest, biggest, and wealthiest organizations in the world. At the beginning, before you are even an ordained deacon, you go through a registration process. You have to give the church all types of information on yourself, including your upbringing, religious and educational background, and physical dimensions, including foot size since all your clothing was to be provided by the Catholic church. Your social security number, and yes of course, your fingerprints were taken and entered into their worldwide database."

"Good, good thinking, Jake, have you reached…"

Jake quickly responded, interrupting Gary before he could finish his sentence. "Yes, we are working with the United States Catholic headquarters. The Basilica of the National Shrine of the Immaculate Conception based in Washington D.C. We should be hearing back shortly if we are able to gain access."

Jake's phone rings. "Detective Blevins here." His eyes widened while looking at Gary, but soon narrowed with disappointment. "Yes, okay, please keep searching and let us know if you find anything. Okay, goodbye."

"Who was that?"

"That was the FBI. They heard back from both the NCAA and the USOC. They have completed a ninety-seven percent search of the databases. Nothing to be found. No matches."

Hours passed. Jake leans back in his chair with his feet up on the desk and has a straw sticking out of his mouth pointing up towards the ceiling. His hands are clasped behind his head as he contemplates his next move. Being run down and working on no sleep, the thoughts on an adequate next move aren't coming as fluidly as he would have liked. His phone rings. He makes no movement other than flicking the straw back and forth with his teeth and tongue. The ringing continues.

"Jake, your phone is ringing."

"Yea, yea." Planting his feet on the floor with a thud, he simultaneously spits the straw out of his mouth, landing it on the crumb-laced sandwich wrapping paper left over from lunch. He grabs the receiver. "Yep!" he answers disparagingly. "Yes, this is detective Jake Blevins." He listens and slowly starts to sit up straighter, bringing his posture into form. "Yes, hello, Bishop." Pausing again for a little bit, Jake stands and starts waving to Gary and the other detectives in the room. They all come scurrying over to his desk. He scrunches his shoulder up to hold the phone against his ear as he scribbles some notes down on a coffee stained piece of paper. "Yes, yes, I got it. That is good." Jake's voice is now excitedly responding to the Bishop. "Yes, do that please. Send us the last known address. We will start looking into them. And again, thank you, Bishop."

"We got a match!" The other detectives look intently at Jake as the sun now glistens through the westward windows, bringing some warmth on their backs. "We have two actually!" Jake exclaimed.

"I don't believe it, but we finally have an ID for our John Doe. His name is Father Thomas Byrne. A priest from Jacksonville, Florida. Four months ago, he was put on leave from his duties as a Catholic priest pending some legal charges. He was a suspect in an investigation on child pornography. The investigation is ongoing, but he has yet to be charged, so he was not fingerprinted by the local police.

"But because of the accusations and the investigation, he was put on leave from the church. He had to move out of the rectory and into a four hundred dollar a month efficiency. He was ordered to have no contact with the Catholic church and to only leave his small apartment for groceries.

"This would explain why no one reported him missing for the last few weeks. He was on his own and no one was looking for him. No one was in daily contact with him. He was basically abandoned by the church and his community after the allegations of his connection with child pornography came about."

"Okay," Gary said. "Now we are getting somewhere. Let's get our second forensics team to make a trip over to Jacksonville and turn that efficiency upside down for clues."

A yet to be seen excitement had overtaken the investigation room as the adrenalin rushed through the veins of all involved.

"What about the second match?"

"Our partial prints! We have an exact match to a Father James Gallagher out of Paterson, New Jersey."

"New Jersey!" Christine stated inquisitively, crunching her eyebrows together and up.

"Yes, New Jersey! The Bishop only had a little background information on this guy. He was an active Catholic priest in various dioceses in New Jersey over the past thirty years. Then, five years ago, he felt he had a calling to work more closely with the needy communities in the lower economic cities. He retired from active priesthood and moved to Paterson to immerse himself in that community."

"Could he be a vigilante priest" Gary asked, "taking it upon himself to punish Father Thomas Byrne for his child pornography? It is certainly pointing in that direction."

"Not only did we have a match on the partial prints, but guess what else?"

"What?"

"He is a very active priest who goes to the gym daily. He plays basketball on the streets every day to improve his relationships with the community and gain trust. Not only does he meet some of our profiling characteristics because he is a strong, fit person, but the Bishop still had his physical dimensions on file. He has a size ten and a half shoe."

"That's it! Great work, Jake."

"Ryan, get your FBI counterparts on the phone and tell them to fuel up the jet. Everybody, we have wheels up in 40 minutes. We are going to New Jersey to get our guy. Call ahead to the local FBI field office, start sending them all our information. Have them set up a supplemental investigation room to be used as our command post upon arrival. I do not want any local law enforcement being aware of the situation. The few FBI agents at the New Jersey field office are all the people that need to know right now. We need to absolutely be the first ones on the scene to apprehend this guy. I do not want a repeat of what happened with Terry Schyminski because of that ignorant and egotistical so-called mayor of Tampa Bay."

Six

The sky had darkened over the tri-state area as the jet made its final approach into Teterboro Airport. The team members sit in silence, staring out the windows, taking in the brilliantly lit New York City skyline. The Freedom Tower highlights the view in all its glory, honoring our victims of the September 11th 2001 terrorist attacks. Gary reflects on that fateful day, the powerful sight just reconfirming why he does what he does. Right there and then, he makes a solemn, silent oath to himself that he will put this guy away.

It's just past midnight when the wheels touch down on New Jersey soil. A caravan of black SUVs is loaded up and the team is transported to the local FBI office.

The new investigation room is already set up with photos and notes that were emailed ahead of time. The office is a near perfect replica with the layout of the evidence previously established in Tampa Bay. Taking in a three hundred and sixty view of the office and evidence, Gary takes his usual command and tells everyone to rest up: "Everyone needs to get a few hours of shut eye." The building has multiple couches scattered throughout the main investigation room and adjoining offices. "I want a daylight approach and we need to be at our best to catch this guy. Seven A.M. prep meeting. Get some rest everybody."

As the early morning hours tick by, Gary just laid on a couch. His shoes are off, his sleeves rolled up, and his tie loosened. His right forearm is resting upon his forehead as he stares into the darkness of the ceiling, repeatedly asking himself questions, trying to decipher the killer's motivation. *What is it with that hand?*

* * *

The hot black coffee steams from their cups as Gary leads the team in the discussion about the layout of the building for the last known address of Father James Gallagher. The New Jersey field office FBI agents add their support, giving their local knowledge of the five-block radius surrounding the target. It is a small efficiency apartment. It has one main room; a small bathroom and kitchenette are located off the back corner of that main room. The apartment is located in a rundown section of Paterson, just as most sections of Paterson are struggling financially and seemingly rundown. The room is located on the west side of the building on the fourth floor, the top floor of this building. Three sets of double windows expose the living space to the west.

The building is the tallest for a three-block radius. Gary explains that a seven-story building is located to the west. "Jake, we are going to perch you up on the corner of that roof top with that high-powered rifle of yours. That will put you about three hundred meters away."

"Not a problem, boss, I have taken out targets up to nine hundred meters."

"We are going to situate four blocks away. We will wait there until Jake gets eyes on the apartment and reports back what he can see."

Suited up in their tactical gear, wearing black from head to toe, the Kevlar vested team have their rifles in their hands. They have multiple ammo packs strapped around their bodies as they head out to load up the black SUVs waiting for them in front of the building. The cool morning fall air is a stark contrast to the hot, humid conditions they had been encountering the last few weeks down in Florida. The shadows from the morning light caress the streets intermittently as they are dissected by the sunbeams coming from the east.

Jake hits the streets first, running to his destination with two agents in tow as backup. Not missing a beat, he rushes through the two broken glass doors, making his entrance to the seven-story building, taking the stairs two at time with his rifle strapped to his back. One of the agents stands post at the broken glass doors while the other humps his way up the stairs behind Jake. As Jake enters the rooftop, the second agent stands guard at the entrance, heading right to the southeast corner of the building, Jake immediately takes his position and perches up with his eye in his scope, immediately locating the fourth-floor apartment of the suspect.

Jake starts communicating through his headset.

"I am set and have a visual on the windows. Two of the windows have their shades drawn, limiting my view. The third window is clear and I have about a forty percent view of the living space. There is an unmade single size bed adjacent to a small nightstand with a light. The bed is located against the back wall, which is to the north.

"Alright, now I see two people. One is sitting in a tall barroom type chair. His back is to me. He has a weapon in his right hand and is pointing it towards the floor. He is facing what seems to be a hostage. The hostage is wearing all black. He looks to be a priest because he is wearing a white clergy collar. The priest is sitting in a regular size chair, so he is a little lower than the suspect. The priest is unable to move, his arms are bonded with duct tape in the straight down position. His arms are affixed to the legs of the chair. The hostage is blind folded, and tape is across his mouth.

"There is no movement right now. I only have a visual on the back of our guy's head. I can't see his facial expressions or if he is talking. I have a clean shot and I can take him out right now. We need to save this hostage. On your call, Gary. Just give me the command."

"No, hold tight. Keep the target in your sights. We are mobile and getting into position, we want this guy alive if possible. I want a dozen agents positioned two blocks out, surrounding this building. Christine, Ryan, and two more agents will go in with me on a silent approach. Our vehicles will stay here. We'll make our final approach by foot. I want radio silence except for comms between Jake and myself."

Gary leads his team of four to the front of the dilapidated building with their guns drawn. One agent runs around back and another agent stands post at the front entrance. Silently they take the stairs to the fourth floor.

"Jake, we are about to enter the fourth-floor hallway. Give us an update."

"I have a clear shot, but there has been no movement."

"Hold strong, Jake."

They enter the water-damaged hallway with the paint peeling away from the walls and ceiling. That damp smell that only inhabits old, unventilated apartment buildings lingers in the air as the three detectives make their way toward the targeted room. Passing two doors, they finally arrive at the last door located down the hall on the west side of the building. With his gun raised up, Gary presses close to the moist wall. He puts his ear up against the door, listening intently for any signs of movement from the inside…no sounds.

In barely a whisper, he says "We want this guy and the hostage alive. Don't shoot, Jake. I repeat, do not shoot."

"Ten four."

"Jake, give me the layout of the room."

"I can't see the door because the first two shaded double windows are limiting my view of the south wall where the door is located. The suspect and the hostage are located on the east wall of the room, about fifteen feet from the southeast corner of the dwelling. The door will open to the inside. Once open, it will give you a direct line of sight to the suspect and the hostage. Take cover when you open the door."

"Ok, we will try and make contact."

Knock, knock, knock. A silent tense pause fills the air. Knock, knock…Gary makes it a little louder now, so it is unmistakably heard.

"Father James! This is detective Gary Hurst. Can we come in?"

"Jake, what do you see? Any movement?"

"No, nothing. Standing strong, waiting on your command."

"Stand strong, we are going to open the door and try to get a close up visual. I am going to try and get him to talk."

Gary stands tall, facing the crack in wooden door that would soon be the opening. His arms are straight out with his gun clutched tight as beads of sweat rest on his forehead. Christine stands to his left while Ryan crouches to the right of the door. Ryan tries the handle. The handle is locked and doesn't move. As silently as possible, Ryan successfully picks the lock. With his left hand on the handle and his gun in his right hand, controlling his breath, he gives an eye signal to Gary and Christine. Gary nods back with affirmation.

Ryan slowly turns the handle. Gary stands in anticipation and visualizes where the suspect is behind the door. He slowly breathes and steadfastly targets that position with his gun.

Barely audible, he says "We are opening the door."

Jake has the suspect's head in his crosshairs, for the suspect has not moved that position since Jake had taken his stance. Jake's gold Catholic cross, glistening in the morning sun, dangles out of his shirt and rests quietly over the polished wooden butt of his rifle.

"We will take him, Jake. Continue to stand strong."

Just as Ryan opens the door, the suspect starts to raise his right arm and hand which is grasping his weapon. Jake reacts, thinking he was raising his gun to shoot the hostage. Within milliseconds, the suspect's gun is almost at head level with the hostage. Ryan swings the door totally open, giving a full visual of the hostage and suspect.

Now, with the suspect's gun aimed right at the hostage's head, Jake squeezes the trigger of his high-powered rifle, sending a slug hurtling towards the suspect's head. Jake lands a direct shot to the back center of the suspect's head.

Gary, still in his stance, clearly witnesses the bullet exploding through the suspect's head. The bullet splatters his face all over the hostage, his blood exploding all over the wall and floor behind the hostage. The hostage's body shadows a bloody outline on the wall as if it were a painting on canvas.

Silence follows the diminishing echo of the gunshot ringing through the run-down buildings of the New Jersey city. Standing in almost disbelief of what just happened, the team of three enters the apartment with guns drawn, quickly clearing the blind corners, kitchenette, and bathroom. Christine rushes to the blood covered hostage to check for vitals…nothing. He was dead.

Incredulousness and confusion go through the detectives' minds as they stand next to the unrecognizable remnants of the human head that moments before sat atop the body that was believed to be the killer. Standing in the center of the small room, Gary examines the now-dead body.

He comes to the quick conclusion that they had been set up. He looks up to the ceiling, viewing a pulley system which had manipulated the dead body. The right hand and arm have a barely visible wire attached to them. The wire is strung from the ceiling through a pulley, which leads to the southwest corner of the room. That part of the room is hidden from Jake's view. The pulley is manipulated with a counterweight and attached to the door, so that when the door opened it displaced the counterweight and the wire lifted the suspect's arm holding the gun. This made it look as though he was going to shoot the hostage, prompting the engagement of Jake's response, falsely luring him to shoot and kill the suspect.

Out of breath and running through the entrance of the door, Jake quickly realizes the result of his actions. In silence, he is distraught and frustrated with himself. Being fooled into taking a human life does not sit well with the young detective.

Gary ponders the crime scene. *This is such a game to our killer. Again, he fabricated a very intricate and detailed plan. Playing us as pawns in his scheme to do his dirty work. Let's look more into this Father James Gallagher. Why him? Why did he have us kill him? What about this so-called hostage? Who is this guy? He is cold to the touch. He only had a very small area of his skin exposed, he is wearing long sleeves, and blindfolded. With all the duct tape, we did not notice how pale white his skin was. He must have been dead for days now.*

Bringing his voice to life, Gary shouts "Get the forensics up here ASAP, I want Alan and his team working this scene two minutes ago!"

"Jake, look at this!" Gary points with a pen in order not to disturb the evidence as he draws Jake's attention to the hands of the duct taped hostage. "Both of his hands seem to be in the same position as our first victim's hand. The middle, ring, and pinky fingers are fixed to his palm, with the index and the thumb left to be in a more-straight position. No coincidence here. This is definitely the work of our guy."

A soft ring from a phone can be heard, but Gary is deep in thought trying to process the thinking that would motivate someone to set them up like this, trying to figure out how and why someone would go through all the planning and execution to make this happen. The ring becomes slightly louder.

Jake, barely able to speak because of his distress, utters the words, "Gary, you going to answer that? Gary, your phone is ringing."

"Oh, yes, I got it." He reaches into his pocket and retrieves his old-school flip phone.

"Detective Gary speaking … hello is anyone there?"

After a pause, a slight, very controlled exhalation becomes audible through the phone. The breathing repeats itself, but still no voice. "Can I help you?" Gary says into the phone, with the intent of having that be his last effort to accept the call.

"DETECTIVE GARY." A very dark and direct voice with eerie undertones finally responds, followed by more deep breathing.

"Yes, this is he. Can I help you?" He now perked up to attention.

In that same very driven voice, the caller asks "I am not sure, but maybe. How could you have just let that happen?"

"Let what happen? Who is this?"

"You know who this is, Gary. Can I call you Gary?"

"Yes, you can call me Gary. What should I call you?"

"I do believe you may be looking for me?" Gary's eyes widen, dilating his pupils as he swiftly turns and starts snapping his fingers at Jake to get his attention, pointing at the phone with exhilarated excitement. Jake moves close to Gary to listen in on the conversation coming from the phone that Gary holds to his ear. With Gary's adrenaline rushing through his veins, the sweat on his forehead gains momentum and starts sliding down his face.

"Why is it that you think I may be looking for you?"

"Come on now, Gary. As this continues to play out, and if you actually think you are going to have the slimmest chance to catch me, you better start giving me more credit than that."

Now the entire team has gathered close trying to transcribe what was barely audible to them as the conversation continues. There's no speaker on Gary's flip phone.

"Ok, why is it that you are calling me?"

"I just wanted to see how your young partner Jake is feeling?"

All the detectives react with a startled look in their eyes.

"With all your knowledge, wisdom, and experience, it seems as though your Catholic cross wearing partner may have just blown the head off an innocent person…or maybe not so innocent. That's for you to find out. Could you enquire with your partner just how he might feel? Did it feel good? I want to know if it felt good. I have always had a feeling of gratification after a kill. It is quite the unique feeling. Is Jake experiencing the same?"

Gary takes a deep breath as he realizes the weight of knowing that the killer they are looking for has just called him on his personal phone. He has direct knowledge of the raid they just conducted and the chaos that had ensued. It has not even been ten minutes, if that.

Gary's memory flashes back to the photo board of evidence. Trying to be as connected to this man as possible, he calms his heartbeat and responds.

"He's obviously feeling lousy. Shaken to the core, like he wants to throw up."

"No Gary, I want you to ask him."

"Jake, how do you feel?"

Jake, without any conviction in his voice, shakes his head up and down and says, "Yes, I feel manipulated and I feel like I want to throw up."

"Interesting. That is good I guess. He has feeling and emotion. As for me, this is not the case. As much as I can honor your efforts in trying to catch me, I could not really care about the person's head that Jake just destroyed. Actually, I am quite appreciative of the enhanced entertainment factor that this has brought to the table. Please extend my gratitude to Jake and your team."

"Why don't you tell me your name?"

"Relax, Gary, all in due time."

Gary knows he must keep this guy on the phone as long as possible. He starts asking questions.

"Then why don't you tell me a little about yourself?"

"Why? To see if I match some cliché profile you initially made as you studied the body hanging far above the 70,000 people in the Tampa Bay Rays' stadium? The body that had just exuded its last few drops of life down onto the pitcher?

"Let's see, what is it that you want me to say? Do you want

to know if my Mommy and Daddy loved me or not? Do you want to know what I think of women? Well, that's easy. As far as women go, I can tell you that I am a big fan. I always have been. They are immensely intriguing. So much so that I think you should know this little fact about me. That when I see a woman in public, I walk closer to her so I can smell her pussy. I can, you know. I can smell their pussies. It gives me great insight into the depth of their soul. It helps me realize who they actually are. And no, they don't all smell the same. Do you ever do that, Gary?"

A long silence.

"Come on Gary, if you want me to talk you are going to have to play along as well. You need to answer my questions. If not, I might as well hang up."

"Wait, wait…No, I do not try to do that."

"Do what? What is the matter? Can't you say it? I want you to say it, Gary."

"No, I do not try and smell them."

"Nope. Not good enough." The deep and powerful voice exclaims. "It looks as though I must be going."

Hastily Gary blurts out…"No, I do not try and smell their pussies!"

Silence follows…then deep breaths as the killer relishes his small victory of getting Gary to say it out loud.

"You probably think I am some middle-aged white guy. Thinking 'OH! He must like it by now. You know, like killing by now. He's got a real taste for it.' Blah blah blah…so cliché, Gary.

"You are going to need to be at the top of your game to

catch me. In all your years of homicide and apprehending your killers, I guarantee you have never met anyone like me. GARY (with the ever-resounding voice now pounding through the phone, with the utmost conviction), I am the most extraordinary and eccentric individual, that maybe, just maybe, you might have the dubious honor of meeting one day, but I doubt it. Oh, look at that, the time has come to end our call. Don't bother trying to trace this call. Somehow, I know you will waste your time anyway."

"No, No, don't go yet," Gary begs.

"Until the next time."

The call ends. Silence ensues as the phone connection disappears.

Gary yells "Get this phone to the station and start seeing what we can do about tracing that call. Go, go, go, every second counts…move it!"

Still standing in the middle of the bloody room with the two bodies positioned like a photo from an old mob killing, Gary turns his attention to the bank of windows letting in the light. He slowly walks over and gazes at all the buildings and windows within his line of view.

"This son of bitch not only set us up, but he watched the entire escapade play out. He was getting off on it. He savored every minute. Every ounce of anticipation was reveled in for the execution of his plan."

Jake, still reeling from all that has happened, starts running for the door.

"He's here. Somewhere, somewhere he's watching us. I'm going to get this guy."

Calmly, Gary, still staring out the window, says in a softer, relaxed voice, "No. Don't bother."

"What!" Jake yells back uncontrollably.

"Don't bother," Gary says. "He's gone, long gone. He watched you kill for him. Now he is on his way. This was his entertainment for today. He had it all planned. He knew exactly how and when he would have to be out of sight."

Seven

Her left cheek lays on the smoothness of the stain-finished, old wooden floor. She's directly in the middle of the dimly lit room. The dark strands of her more than shoulder-length hair are strewn up above her head, flowing ever so gently on the floor. Her brown eyes are now softly covered by their lids. Her breathing is slow and calm. There is a little bit of saliva drooling from her funny-shaped, apple red colored lips. It leaves a tiny puddle on the floor next to her pale, warm skin. Her arms are outstretched and taut as her wrists are cuffed in two-inch wide metal bracelets. The bindings are secured by a thick heavy chain that is anchored deep into the polished wooden floor with a thick metal plate and massive screws.

Her usually luscious white breasts are now pressed flat against the front panel of the dark leather couch. The bones of her spine can be followed up her bare back as it bridges over the leather cushions of the couch, placing the curvature of her hips directly over the top of the couch. Her ankles are placed far apart, enclosed with the same wide metallic cuffs, spreading the silhouette of her long legs down the back side of the couch. They are moored securely to the floor with such a tightness that it allows for maybe only a few centimeters of movement, if any at all.

The high-ceilinged room has almost no decorations minus a few antiques. The old figures find a home on the mantle of the oversized fireplace about fifteen feet from the back side of the couch. The aged room has a warmth overtaking it as the blue-orange wood fire casts its shadows across the floor.

"Ok, ok, ok…just a little pin prick…There'll be no more aaaaaaaahhhh!…But you might feel a little sick," from the song "Comfortably Numb" by Pink Floyd, blares at an almost unbearable decibel level. The music brings a blanket of calm ecstasy and joy to the space. It is a feeling which is only felt by a few in this world. It settles itself on the dark figure looming back and forth between the raging fireplace and the innocence that is sprawled over the couch in front of him.

The outline of the body stands at over six foot five inches tall. The demeanor reflects that of a person who has the strength that only comes from tapping deep inside their inner soul. The unhurried pacing of the beastlike man is followed only by the shadows on the floor and the movement of his black hair. His thick, shoulder-length hair moves ever so slightly right below his shoulders. As the shadows of the impressive athletic specimen reach the edges of the floor, they pause ever so slightly before creeping their way back. His naked, slightly sweat soaked skin, is glistening from the light of the fire and the moon. The moon light is scantily shining through a stained-glass window on the far wall. He breathes the air with such intent. It is a breath showing the depth of a person relishing in a greatness only found beyond our world.

His near erect red penis is starting to throb. With his eyelids partially covering the clear sky blues eyes beneath them, he continues his pacing right behind the beauty of the girl in front of him, breathing with an anticipation, waiting as the moment builds, the moment in time that lines up with the stars shining deep within the universes. Then, and only then, does our man stop pacing and settles his dramatic figure right behind the unmoving, slow breathing woman on the couch. The light of the fire casts its light around him. He has an awareness of his surroundings like no other.

With the music still blaring, the focus of the room is on the man's breathing. His eyes are closed now as he draws deep, meditative, belly breaths. In through his nose and out through his mouth. He detects the fresh aroma of the woman humped over the couch in front of him, taking the smell of her pussy into the deepest crevices of his lungs and brain. Opening only a sliver of his eyelids, he admires the vulnerability of the woman. With the vision of her black pussy hair laying gently around her pink opening, and the anticipation of what is to be brings his cock to full erection.

He leans to the left to grab a chain dangling from the ceiling and wraps it around his hand and wrist. Leaning ever so slowly and out stretching his arm to the right, he secures himself with another chain. The now immense figure takes on the unmistakable shape of a cross. As he stands with the warmth of the fire blazing upon his backside, he slowly starts to sway from side to side. He brushes his long blood-filled shaft softly across the left white hip of the beauty in front of him. Slightly wetting it on her pinkness as he brings it across her backside, giving him that arousing, ever so unforgettable skin on skin feeling. Back and forth he slowly moves his now throbbing red penis across her skin, her flowing juices moistening his skin more and more with each passing.

After much suspense, he stabilizes his body directly behind her. He lines up his bulging cock and slowly slides it into her, leaving himself deep inside her as the exquisiteness of the moment flows through him. He waits with patience before he starts thrusting, then thrusts with an unprecedented power to continue his penetration deep inside of her, filling her hole with all of himself. Biding his time, he drives the crescendo. His sweat dances down his chest and over his nipples. As he drives back and forth, his heavy ball sack pounds against her, tantalizing her sensitive clit. The chains are rattling, but are unheard because of the massive volume of the music. Her legs start to quiver as moisture pools on the floor beneath them.

In the warm darkness of this room, only these two know how long the time has been passing. This moment is to be valued and honored. It is not an instant too soon that he embarks on the release of his warmth that fills her deep inside.

Eight

The darkness of a very dimly lit examination room encompasses the three dead victims. The naked, dead body of Father Gallagher, with a fleshy crater of mush remaining where his face once was, lays cold on the stainless-steel bed. He has only about sixty percent of his skull barely attached to his neck. A small table with a blue surgical cloth draped over it sits next to the body. The table has the fragments of Gallagher's nose, teeth, tongue and eyelids. The remnants are placed out in such a way to try and piece back together the puzzle of what was once his face.

Gary stands with his team waiting for Alan to finish up the final details of his report on the latest two victims, Father James Gallagher and John Doe number two.

"Alan, our dead bodies are mounting up!"

"Yes, they certainly are. We had our first victim, Father Thomas Byrne, along with the rest of our tangible evidence, transported overnight to our new headquarters here in New Jersey.

"Well we can start with this one, Father James Gallagher. Obviously, we thought he was our suspect, but he turned out to be another victim. His time of death is being placed at the moment Detective Jake's bullet pierced the back of his skull, causing instant death. He was alive up to the point, just highly sedated. Doped up on oxycontin and other opiates, which is why he was not moving much or saying anything.

"These ligature marks around his torso, legs, ankles, and left arm are where he was bound to the high barstool. The killer used very strong but clear and almost invisible wire to tie him up. Knowing very well that he had to keep his sedated victim in the upright position, the killer used this steel bar to keep him sitting upright. It was attached to his back under his shirt, aligning his spine and neck in the upright position so as not to slouch. His eyes were epoxied open using the same epoxy found on victim number one's fingers and hand.

"The killer had two means of administering the opiates to this victim. First, he intravenously injected him with a needle directly into the carotid artery. But as far as I can see, this method was only used once. My guess is that he used this first method when he initially captured him. This would be the quickest and most effective way to sedate the victim for control.

"The second method was sublingual, the same method which was used on our first victim, which makes me guess that he also used the intravenous method to the carotid artery on our first victim as well. It is just that the injection point was undetectable due to the murder weapon being implanted right into the same spot as the injection point.

"Our killer must have been on site, attending to and doping this victim every six to eight hours around the clock. He would have had to keep him under the proper sedation."

The attention of the room turns to John Doe number two, who unlike the other victims, is face down on the cold stainless-steel table. Alan starts to get a little emotional as he wipes his nose and eyes to compose himself and restore his professionalism.

"I just must reiterate—after examining this poor soul, I am almost at a loss for words. My faith in humanity has been shaken to the core. Team, we have a truly sick psychopath running loose, the sickest I have ever encountered in my thirty years of working homicide and medical examination.

"I put the time of death approximately six to seven days prior to our raid, give or take two to three days. The body was either put on ice or refrigerated for preservation, making it more difficult to narrow down an exact time of death. He was dead for days, maybe even a full week, before we came along.

"He was bound with an inordinate amount of duct tape to the lower sitting chair in the room. He was bound just like our first victim, Father Thomas Byrne, was in the stadium. Even though he was already dead, the amount of duct tape alone helped keep his posture in a more upright position. As noticed at the crime scene, both of his arms were taped down to the sides of the chair, with his hands epoxied in the same formation as our Father Byrne. His pinky, ring, and middle finger affixed to his palm, making a cylindrical shape between his fingers and his hand, leaving his index and thumb to continue out as straight.

"He has the same intravenous injection mark on his carotid artery, but no indication of sublingual ingestion of opiates. When compared to our other two victims, there was only a small amount of opiates found in his system, so he was most likely only sedated once upon his capture.

"It was obvious upon the initial examination that cause of death was exsanguination; in other words, he bled out. The pale color of his skin is the primary indicator, but as I was examining him face up, I could not conclude how he bled out. As I turned him over, we found this massive bruising around his anus. The anus was brutally penetrated and torn apart by some very long object, but I do not know what.

"Upon further examination, I noticed whatever the object was, it left a similar octagonal footprint as the entry wound on our first victim. Penetrating to the same twelve-inch depth, piercing the small and the large intestines, then the pancreas while the end of this object reached all the way to the stomach.

There is indication of a long and prolonged exsanguination, with massive trauma around all the internal organs. Even just inserting and removing an object up through the anus, and allowing it to bleed out, would take more than an hour before death occurred. The killer probably left the object inserted in place to slow the blood flow down even more, purposely increasing the duration of torture and ultimate death. The trauma to the inner organs was a result of moving the object back and forth while it was inserted."

Who is this guy? Where did this all happen? Gary ponders the questions.

* * *

Nine days earlier.

Standing in the shadows of the autumn night, our killer stands out of sight in the corner of a Knights of Columbus parking lot in south Jersey. He has a deepness to his breath which is visible as it exudes out of his lungs and mouth. He waits patiently for his intended victim to depart the building. The victim is the sole person left cleaning up after a men's only Wednesday night social group meeting.

As Father Eric walks in the cool air across the parking lot he carries a large box with Styrofoam cups and all the fixings to make a large batch of coffee. He comes up against his fifteen-year-old blue four-door car, leaning the box up against the door and his hip as he fumbles for the keys in his pocket to unlock his car.

Out of the darkness comes a needle that dives deep into his carotid artery. The killer plunges the needle into his neck and delivers the opiates right into his bloodstream. It has the instant desired effect of sedation. Dropping his box and falling backwards, Father Eric is only supported by our killer who grabs under the priest's arms. The killer picks up the keys, unlocks the doors and maneuvers his victim into the back seat of the car.

Pulling out a large roll of duct tape, he binds his hands behind his back, tapes his ankles, and puts tape across his mouth and eyes. He covers the limp body of the priest with an old woolen blanket that is on the seat. The opiate injection has left the victim fully sedated. He has drifted away without an ounce of struggle put up against his attacker.

Our killer throws the once dropped box, cups, and coffee

contents into the trunk of the car and gets in the driver seat. He embarks on the long two and half hour drive to his destination, taking back roads all the way.

Nearing his arrival, the killer drives past the many mansions in the heights. Even though the leaves have started to fall, he notices the absence of even one windblown, orange-tipped red leaf on any of the manicured lawns. Taking in the silence, he slowly drives through the twenty-five mile per hour wealthy suburb. He takes a left into his long driveway and hits the garage door opener. Only one of the three heavy wooden doors, braced with custom black iron fixtures along the front, rises to exposes the three thousand square foot, impeccably clean garage. He drives in. There are only two vehicles parked in the garage. The first is a dark brown van. The second is a nineteen fifties, hard top, red Corvette. With only the two cars present, there is ample room to park the old blue sedan in the corner of the garage. It is out of the view from the street, even if any of the garage doors were to open.

* * *

Time has passed into the dark, early morning hours. With a string of opiate-induced drool hanging from the bottom of his lip as his head bobs in and out of consciousness, the victim's heavy eyes finally find some strength to open, trying to focus. A blurry candle sits in the distance. As it comes more into view, he lifts his head and starts to realize his most unfortunate situation. He glances around at the stone walls and cement floor. He finds only light from the array of candles scattered through the fairly large room. There is a single chair spaced about fifteen feet from where he is. The closed off room, with only one door, is situated in the middle of the basement in the large mansion, hence not a window is to be found.

Being only five foot eight inches tall, Father Eric realizes his vantage point is about a foot higher than it would be if he were standing. He is not standing. He is situated quite awkwardly, as if a very young child sat on the toilet without the seat down. He is strapped into a tall, pyramid-type contraption supported with three large ten by ten-inch timber posts. The seat-like wooden top of the pyramid is where he is duct taped in. He is so tightly secured, with a very tight fit, that he cannot move anything other than his head.

As he notices his knees are tight to his chest, he realizes he has no clothes on. His view is from his knees down to his bare feet directly in front of him. His pale, meek shoulders are on top of the fixture, with his arms strapped in front of him straight across the bottom of his legs. His hands are bound to his ankles. His torso and upper legs are dropped right through the hole.

This position is exposing his white ass, with barely a set of balls squeezing through his two legs that are pressed so tightly together. The predicament has his anus unnaturally spread apart. His open anus is now the lowest part of his body, directly facing the floor. The separation of the three wooden posts gives a clear opening to the vulnerability of his body from all sides. The rather long foundations, topping off at well over six feet, are based with wheels to make the apparatus mobile.

Panic has set in for the Father. Sweating from the effects of the opiates and his dire situation, he starts to mumble in prayer...our father who art in heaven, hallowed be thy name, thy will be done...Becoming more aware of his surroundings, he begins to dial into a faint, but heavy, deep breathing sound coming from the far dark corner behind him.

Stuttering. "Who...who...is there? Is someone there? Help me, please help me. What is going on? Why am I here?"

A long time passes. There are only a few sounds to be heard. The deep breathing coming from the corner, the Father's tearful cries and screeches, and the faint flicker of the candles illuminating the room all fill the dwelling with sound.

Now that he is coming out of his opioid-induced sedation, the prolonged pause without any answer or action has bought our father to a level of distress that he has never known. He is fearing for his life.

A deep, controlled voice beckons from the dark corner. "What is that you are saying? Is that a prayer? Who are you speaking to in your prayer?"

"Yes...Yes." The priest finally composes himself enough to answer. "I am praying, I am praying to God."

"God...who is your god?"

"My God is the Catholic God, the Father, the Son and the Holy Spirit."

Taking his time, our killer confidently strides out of the shadows, giving the Father his first glimpse of him. The flickering shadow of the candles waver over the strong chin, high cheekbones, and protruding brow. The killer has the most intriguing, lightest color of blue eyes that are transfixed on the fear-filled look of Father Eric. Down the right side of the killer's body, the veins of his forearm are pulsing as he grips the heavy twenty-one-inch sword-like weapon.

"Tell me, what is your god saying?" No answer. "I said, what is your god saying? You are talking to him, aren't you? If this is the all-powerful Catholic god, the one you have so praised and preached of for most of your adult life, why wouldn't he be answering you? I can't hear anything. I wonder if you should keep praying?"

Facing each other, the killer and Father Eric only have about a foot of space between their faces.

"Do you remember me?"

"No," he says, weeping. "No, I don't know who you are."

"I disagree. You damn well know who I am. You definitely know who I am and I know who you are. It has been some time, but you know me all too well *Deacon* Eric."

Father Eric's eyes widen as he tries to gulp whatever moisture he had left in his throat. He pisses himself from fear as he realizes the identity of his captor.

"I do believe with complete conviction, that you are praying to the wrong god. I know this from experience. As once long ago, I myself, was in a predicament much like you. I prayed out to this same god of yours, just as I was instructed to do by all of you priests. In both good times and in times of need, we should pray, that is what you all said. Well, I was in dire need just like you are now. But there was no answer to my prayers. No savior came. No saving from god for little me."

As the fear of death oozes from his pores, there is no misconception of the unspeakable situation he is now being faced with. The priest starts to plead.

"Please, please help me? Please, please don't kill me?" he blubbers like a toddler who did not get what he wanted, barely able to breathe and speak at the same time. "Please don't kill me."

"Why? You are supposed to be a man of god. Are you not a man of god? Are you not ready for death? *For isn't it upon dying that one awakens to eternal life?* ISN'T IT? That is what you preach. Yes, maybe you are finally realizing it is all some sort of charade. Your god, your church, your false values and convictions, your whole life … it is all just a façade."

Letting some time pass, the killer now asks with a vengeance "Why is it that you did not help me when you had the chance?"

"I do not know."

"Again I ask, why is it that you took no action in my time of need?"

Stumbling over his words, "I... I … dunno."

"WRONG ANSWER."

Putting his right foot back a little, the killer braces his stance. He draws his right arm backward past his hip and with the power deep within his core, he violently thrusts the weapon up and inside the Father's anus.

The priest's head snaps backwards as he feels the unprecedented pain. He squeals for help. The victim is helpless to move and has no options but to be totally aware of the pain and torture being inflicted upon him.

The killer leaves about twelve inches of the weapon inserted in the priest's anus. The cross bar and handle of the weapon are hanging from his ass. There is barely a drop of blood, for the large instrument is holding it all inside of the helpless man.

Pacing around the pyramid, the killer patiently allows time to pass. He wants to allow for the maximum deliverance of this pain. The killer wants him to feel it all. He needs him to take it all in.

"It is a pretty straightforward question, don't you think? I say, why is it that you did not help me in my time of need? Isn't that what Catholic priests dedicate their lives to? Is that not your mission? To help people?"

"I do not know," Eric weeps.

Backing up and taking a field goal kicker's three step approach, the killer, with his black Doc Martens, swiftly kicks the handle of the sword-like weapon which is protruding from Eric's ass. Coming from the depth of his soul, he belts out, "WRONG ANSWER."

"What were you so scared of? What fear did you have that made you freeze in your tracks, and not help me? Was the fear worse than the fear you have right now?"

"No, this fear is worse."

"Ah yes, now maybe we are getting somewhere. Finally, an honest answer. What was it then that you feared?"

"I feared the wrath of the priest. I feared he would ruin all that I was working towards. That he would bring an end to my life as I knew it. It was the only life I knew and that I ever wanted. To be a servant of the Catholic church."

"So, so selfish. Don't you see the hypocrisy in your thinking?"

"Yes, I see it now. I should have helped you. I should have stood up for you and fought for you. I should have never left."

With a rage of disgust, our killer swiftly kicks the handle of the sword again, slowly tearing apart the insides of the Father.

The priest is enduring a very slow death. Despite the trauma being delivered, it will not bring on his death any quicker. The weapon is doing its job by holding all his blood inside. The killer is circling his victim and breathing deep. He is relishing in the moment, enjoying the infliction of the long-overdue punishment which is being bestowed upon this man. Once again, the killer starts to hear a mumbling.

"Hail Mary, full of grace, the Lord is with thee, blessed art thou among women, and blessed is the fruit of thy womb, Jesus. Holy Mary, Mother of God, pray for us sinners, now and at the hour of death…"

"Are you actually praying? Really?"

"Yes, I am."

"To that same Catholic god that is not going to come knocking anytime soon?"

"Yes, yes I am."

"Maybe you should try another god. It seems like you should be praying to me." In the deepest tone of his resounding voice. "I, ME…I am the only GOD present in this situation. The god you have wasted so much time preaching about and praising is not going to answer you just like he did not answer me. Please tell me, how does that feel?"

After a long pause, no answer is given as the pain and desperation of the situation has overtaken any strength or will this man once had. He is broken. There is no more mumbling. No more of the desperate crying out in prayer.

"I am your God now. I am the one with all the power, I am

the one who makes the rules. I will make the decision. I will make your death happen when I decide. In my time and only my time do things happen."

Pacing with light beads of sweat laying on his skin, the killer steps back and gives another powerful thumping kick to the now bloody handle of the weapon, sending unimaginable shards of pain deep within the Father. His eyes become heavy from the pain as his head drops forward lost in unconsciousness. Walking slowly across the candle lit room, the killer takes his place in the chair. With both hands he runs his fingers through his thick black hair, getting it out of his face, as he sits back to watch the slow drip of blood hit the floor underneath the slowly dying man.

Hours will slip away as the killer occasionally slaps the face of the father to bring him back to the reality of his pain. Waiting with the patience of only someone that is driven from a vengeance, the killer watches and takes pleasure in the much deserved, unhurried death of Father Eric.

* * *

I agree, Alan. Our guy is a psychopath. He is relinquished from all feelings, emotions, and sympathy for his victims. He has no qualms about his actions. We need to find out what made him this way.

Nine

Standing inside the drab, off white walls that enclose the local FBI office, which is now the headquarters of this investigation, the team thumbs through pictures and paperwork on their desks. The timeline and victims' photos now fill the first two whiteboards and spread over to the third.

"Ok, let's get a handle on this."

Standing at the front of the room, gesturing to the whiteboards surrounding them, Gary starts leading the discussion.

"What is all this evidence telling us? What is it that we know about the victims? And what is it that we know about our killer? What theories do we have as a motive? What created him? What do we know from his phone call? Who, where, when, and how do we think he will kill again?"

Eager to get the morning going, Jake jumps into the discussion. "He is meticulous. He is carefully planning out his story, making his statements in very big way as he kills. He has to be educated. Hacking the computers for the CCTV and the air system in the Tampa Bay Stadium tells us he has had a high level of education, either at an institution level or self-taught. Many hackers are self-taught to stay off the grid. He hasn't made a mistake — the only clues left behind were intentional, pretty easily leading us to Gallagher and setting us up. Then of course he called. Man, he is smug."

Christine chimes in, which starts the discussion coming from everyone. "We have three dead Catholic priests. It is like he has a vengeance. His motive could be revenge."

"We know our first victim, Father Thomas Byrne, was awaiting trial for child pornography, maybe our killer was a victim? It seems like every few months, we have a different Catholic church being exposed for preying on and sexually abusing children over the past 75 years."

"Yes, yes, that could be a connection."

"Why game one of the World Series? What is the significance of having that be his first kill? He wanted a big stage. He wanted the biggest audience available. He wants to be known. Ok, well what about the configuration of the hands? There has to be something to that."

Gary takes the lead of the discussion. "Maybe it wasn't his first kill. That is a very big stage for his first ever kill! Let's start tracking down background information on what we do have. Ryan and Christine, find out what you can about the duct tape and epoxy that he is using. Is it a specific brand and where can it be purchased?

"I know it's a needle in the haystack, but start researching higher education institutions, in particularly those with highly accredited IT programs. Narrow your search to the northeast, targeting the Ivy League schools and the smaller liberal arts schools up in New England. Start canvassing the professors and the heads of the IT departments. Look for extremely bright individuals that were off the charts in their ability. I know all those students in those schools are exceptional, but we are looking for a standout, someone who is head and shoulders above the rest, even amongst the brightest students. He was definitely an introvert who kept to himself, not very social and probably only spoke to people when he was spoken to.

"Jake, a few items for you to follow up on. I want you on top of finding out what type of murder weapon he could be using. Then, check in with the guys trying to trace the phone call. Find out if we have broken the code for the CCTV footage from the stadium. We have to be able to get something from that.

"I will get a crew of local FBI agents and unis to start profiling all the Catholic churches in the tri-state area. We need a list of which ones have had even an inkling of an accusation of sexual abuse anywhere in their history. We need to get names and last known address of all the altar boys in every one of those churches."

"Gary did you..."

"Yes, they got me a new up-to-date iPhone and it has a working speaker. To be prepared if our guy calls again, they have programmed it to immediately start recording any phone call that comes to that number."

Grabbing Gary's elbow, Jake pulls him off to the side to have more of a private conversation.

"Gary, how does this sit with you? Like you, I was also raised a strict Catholic. Now we are tracking a serial killer that is taking out Catholic priests. For crying out loud, he set me up to kill one of them."

"That isn't your fault, Jake, you need to let that go. No, it doesn't sit very well with me at all. This one bothers me more than most of the serial killers I've tracked and caught over the past thirty years. It makes me queasy when I wake up and it stays with me until I sleep, if you want to call it sleep. It's almost as bad as what happened with Tristan Colburn." Complete sadness envelopes Gary.

"Colburn, that was over twenty years ago for you, one of your first big homicide cases. I know we are new partners and have never spoken about that. But I just need to say that was completely tragic and I have such immense respect for you regarding how you handled that and how you have moved on. I don't think I could do the same."

"Moved on? Never really moved on. Life just kept happening and I just kept getting older. But no, I don't think I can say I ever moved on. It still lives with me every day."

"We need to catch this guy. This is on a whole other level. It is past getting personal with me."

"Yes, Jake, I agree, this one is different also."

As the hours close in on the day, Jake spends his time sitting at his desk, perusing all weapons or swords with a length of twelve inches or more, going through the FBI database of murder weapons and doing an intensive web search. He views hundreds upon hundreds of objects from ancient to modern times. The uniqueness of the octagonal shape leads him to a dead end every time. He can't find anything that could replicate their murder weapon. It has to be strong and dense enough to uphold its shape while it penetrates the victims. It is not a sword-like, thin blade, but something very thick, which cancels out most weapons in the database or on the web.

His desk phone rings.

"Jake here."

"Hey Jake, this detective Tom from the IT lab. I am following up on your CCTV investigation."

"Yea, Tom, what have you found?"

"Unfortunately, we still have not broken into this guy's hack. He is one of the best in the world. He is brilliant in regard to how he hacked this system and how he has blocked anyone from getting in to see that footage. We have our best FBI guys working on it. We are also reaching out to the CIA to use their resources."

"What about the phone trace?"

"Well, we found out what he is doing, kind of. He uses a computer program to bounce the call from cell phone to cell phone, using up to ten burners to bounce the call through."

"Ok, so where does it start then?"

"That's just it. He starts the call from an untraceable Wi-Fi IP address. All it does is send you on a wild goose chase until we somehow maybe crack that IP address."

"Thanks for the update, Tom. This case takes precedent over everything else. Stay on your team and keep chasing that goose. We have to find him."

Gary looks over from across the room with an inquisitive look, hoping for something, some good news, some type of lead to go on. But Jake shakes his head back and forth.

"Nope, nothing. They can't trace the call and they can't break the code for the CCTV footage. At least we were right about something. This guy is smart and extremely educated. He knows his stuff about information technology and hacking."

"What about the phone trace?" Gary asks.

"He has us good, Gary. It's just a shell game. Once you think you have one pinpointed, you realize it isn't it, and you start chasing the next one. All dead ends so far."

Christine perks up from her desk, "We identified the brand name of the duct tape and epoxy being used. All the samples match up from the different crime scenes. They are the most basic common brand of both duct tape and epoxy. They can be purchased at thousands and thousands of stores across America, as well as online. Home Depot, Lowes, Target, Wal Mart, any hardware store or almost any basic supermarket and convenience store in every small and big town. But we need much more than that to narrow down the possibilities of where they were purchased. We think our guy probably buys large quantities at a time, stocking up on his supplies to execute his plan. We will start with the big-name stores, asking about anyone, regular joes, contractors, just about anybody who might be buying unusually large amounts of both those items."

As the day slips well into the night, the desk lamps now illuminate the office. Gary reminds them that their killer has not stopped planning. "He is organizing his next kill right now. The anticipation is what is driving him. The game he is playing with us is keeping him engaged and on his toes. He is probably more engaged and excited now than when he started. He wants to win. We have to stop him. We must win this so-called game."

As the team all shake their heads in agreement, Gary tells

them to finish up what they are working on. "It's late. Get some shut eye. We'll meet up at six am tomorrow over breakfast to go over anything new and what our next step is to be."

Ten

As the end of October draws near, most of the leaves have found their way to the ground, with only the rare few remaining up on the branches. The warm sunlight is welcome as it cuts through one of the colder New Jersey mornings to come their way. The booth table is half lit with the beams of sun making their way through the smudges on the windows of the Parkway Diner.

Steam rises from the two freshly poured cups of black coffee that sit in front of Jake and Christine. Working on a few hours of sleep, Christine colors her coffee a light brown as she adds her cream and gently clinks her spoon against the edge of the cup as she stirs it. Brushing the brown hair up and out of her face, which allows the sun to reveal the true-blue color of her eyes, she starts to break the ice with Jake.

"How is that lady friend of yours back in Chicago?"

Staring through the window as if he were looking and searching for Gary and Ryan to pull up into the parking lot, Jake dazes out with the deep thoughts of remorse he is carrying from pulling the trigger on Father Gallagher. Hearing the question, he eases back into reality. "Well, our little venture here, being in Florida and now New Jersey for more than a month, I am pretty sure has sealed our fate. She was on the fence anyway about staying with me because of my line of work. You know the hours and the commitment and dedication we must put into it… it was just too much for her. I don't blame her so much. She is a nice girl, but she wanted something more stable. Someone to be home at five for dinner, someone to take the kids to school in the morning, and shop at Bed Bath and Beyond on the weekends. I just can't give that to her."

"Oh, I didn't know. I'm sorry to hear that."

"Thank you, but no worries. It is better that we know now than later."

"Yes, I agree."

Jake's eyes have now moved from his window gazing to looking at Christine. As they exchange pleasantries, with sun hitting the right side of her face, shining off her brown hair, he sees and starts to realize the true beauty of her eyes and the intriguing depth of the woman that is sitting across from him.

"What about you? How are things between you and Ryan?"

Smirking with a small half smile she says "Ryan, I love Ryan. He is a great partner, but Ryan is gay. We are not together."

"Really! He's gay?"

"Yes! And he is happily married. He and his husband, Jim, have a three-year-old son."

Bells chime over the glass doors of the Parkway Diner entrance as Gary and Ryan walk in to join them in the booth. As Jake and Christine are both bashfully smiling and glancing away from each other, Gary asks "What's so funny? What's so funny at six am at the Parkway Diner?"

Laughing it off, Jake says, "Nothing funny here," as he catches one more glimpse into the eyes of Christine.

The waitress, dressed in a typical, nineteen fifties' brown outfit with pink and white trim, brings two more cups of coffee to the table.

"Good morning everyone, are all of you ready to order?"

Christine orders a half of grapefruit, two scrambled eggs, and wheat toast. Both Jake and Ryan back that up with "Yes, that sounds good, I'll have the same." All eyes turn to Gary as he orders.

"I'll have cheese fries with brown gravy and a double egg, Taylor ham and cheese, with salt-pep-ketch on a hard roll, please."

The other three look at Gary with sarcastically funny judgmental looks.

"What!" Exclaims Gary.

As he starts to smile and laugh a bit, "If you are in New Jersey, you must have a Taylor ham egg and cheese, salt-pep-ketch, with cheese fries. This breakfast is legendary."

For the first time that these four have been together as a team, which is a month now, some small laughter and smiles finally expose themselves in banter. It is a good release of the tension from the stressful case and life in general.

Jake jokes back, "Maybe try some fruit in your diet and you wouldn't be sweating every time we walk up the stairs." Jake's statement garners some more laughs from everyone at the table.

Finishing up his last few gravy-drenched cheese fries, Gary asks the waitress for the bill and requests four more coffees to go. The bells chime when they exit the Parkway Diner and for a moment the mood is light. Making their way down the four slabs that make up the stairs to the parking lot, a faint ringing sound is coming from Gary's top left breast pocket. Fumbling a bit, trying to get a hold of the new larger size iPhone, he finally retrieves it from his pocket. The phone shows unknown as the caller ID. As the team walks a few steps ahead, Gary swipes the screen to answer the call.

"Hello, good morning, this is Gary." The characteristic deep breaths from the first phone call that rests all too clear in Gary's mind resound from the phone as Gary is stopped in his tracks. After a short pause he asks "Hello? Is anyone there?" Gary knows very well that this is their guy. As the other three detectives notice Gary has lost pace behind them, the smiles and lightness of the moment drain into the darkness of the case. They turn to see what is going on. Coming together next to their squad cars, Gary switches to the speaker phone so the team can hear the conversation.

"Yes, Gary, this is your friend calling."

"My friend? I am not sure I could say we are friends at this point. I do not even know your name and I do not know what I am supposed to call you. What should I call you?"

"Well, Gary, for two people to go through such an experience together like the one we are engaged upon, we must be friends. We are certainly bonding. It's inevitable, don't you think?"

"No, I do not think so. Maybe we are getting to know each

other a bit, but I can't say we are friends. Maybe if I knew more about you we could start to become friends. Why don't you tell me a little bit about yourself?"

"What is it you want to know?"

"Well, why don't we start by you talking about your fixation with killing Catholic priests? Are you Catholic?"

"Catholic? Me? Definitely not. Maybe in an earlier life some people tried to get me into that. You know, made me go to church, made me pray. They must have thought it was good for me. But that didn't really work out. Not for me anyway. I'm definitely not Catholic. I know you, and your gold cross-wearing partner Jake, both of you are Catholic. Tell me, Gary, do you still go to church to pray to God? Do you still go to church to confess your sins? Even after the tragic losses in your life, do you still believe in God?"

"Yes, I still believe in God with my whole being. Despite my tragedies, regardless of the bad things that have happened in life, I pray every day and I still go to church. It is my strong faith that still makes everything work for me. I am starting to understand maybe that you do not go to church, but you did at one time. Why don't you tell me about that?"

"Well, yes, that could be interesting. But first, you have to tell me something. How did it make you feel when Muriel's throat was slashed right in front of you?"

The blood from Gary's face rushes to his heart. His face turns white as death. Gulping the dryness that has now set into his mouth, Gary does his best to hold his composure and professionalism.

"It was tragically devastating. It was like losing a limb. No, it was more like losing something that made up half of my soul. It was like the spring losing its flowers for all of eternity."

Reeling in the delight of the conversation, the caller says "Ah…ah yes, thank you so much for sharing. Dreadful, I might add. Losing your wife right in front of you. Even worse that it came at the hands of the killer you were so desperately trying to apprehend. Must be unthinkable."

Gary and his team are dumbfounded at the knowledge the killer has about Gary and the death of his wife. The cause of death for Muriel was sealed in the file and was never made public.

"For eternity? Don't you ever think you will see her again?"

"Well, yes, I do actually. I believe in God. I believe in heaven. I believe in the afterlife. I believe we will be reunited when the time is right."

With the sarcasm running thick, the caller says "Oh, that is so beautiful, Gary. Whatever keeps you going."

Gary tries to turn the conversation back onto the killer. "Ok, now what about you? Why don't you tell me where you used to go to church? I gave you what you wanted, now it's your turn. Tell me about yourself, my friend." Using the term friend, Gary tries to lure the killer into opening up about himself.

"Sounds about right. I'm in. I'll keep up my side of the bargain. I'll tell you a little story. I hope you have some time."

"I have all the time you need."

A brief pause filled with his signature heavy breathing ensues as the killer gathers his thoughts.

"Tiberius was a seemingly happy kid…"

"Tiberius? Is that your name?"

"Gary, please don't be rude, please don't interrupt. We will never get anywhere if you are going to interrupt me every time I start to speak. But yes, you can call me Tiberius.

"As I was saying, at some point in time, Tiberius had a seemingly happy and easy life. At least for a while anyway. His father was very successful financially, so Tiberius did not have any material wants and was being raised in a wealthy suburban town. He had great schools to attend and a multitude of extra-curricular activities to choose from. Tiberius was an only child and did not spend much time with his father. His father spent most of time in the city making money. When the father was home, he spent his time watching sports on TV, waxing his antique car or reprimanding and disciplining Tiberius for not being good enough. He constantly set unreasonable standards for Tiberius to try and attain.

"While the mom was sometimes around, she was a town socialite, spending her time at luncheons and dedicating herself to being at every party or gathering the affluent town had to offer. Drinking her way through the day from mid-morning, to lunch, through dinner, and of course all the nightcaps that followed.

"So, minus the overbearing, uncaring, and absent father, and the drunk mom, it was a seemingly privileged life. He lived in a great big house and had a great town to be a part of. He participated in almost everything that was available to help ward off the lack of a family life. His favorite sport was swimming, which he was pretty good at. Being naturally athletic, he also played baseball and basketball. For all intents and purposes, Tiberius had it good enough to deal with the rigors of his parents.

"As a child, the father attended the Catholic school in town and was a devout lifetime attendee of the Catholic church which resided right across the street. From the start of my schooling, I was forced to attend the Catholic school as well.

"Come to think of it, Gary. I think my father was a lot like you."

"Really, how so?"

"My father believed the Catholic church was the end all be all. It was everything regarding God, spirituality, and all matters regarding what is right and what is wrong in this world. How could the Catholic church or the priests possibly do anything wrong? That was his strong stance on it.

"Following in my father's footsteps, I was forced to be an altar boy. As an eight-year-old, which was the typical age, I started my training. As such, I became very familiar with the outlay of the church, the priest's rectory and living quarters, and of course the sacristy.

"It was in the sacristy that as an altar boy we did the most of our training, becoming familiar with everything necessary to help with the services. The sacristy was a rather large room. The center piece of the room was a very long, wooden, and beautifully refurbished antique cabinet. It was a waist-high, dresser type piece of furniture. This large piece housed most of the items needed for mass services, baptisms, weddings, and of course funerals: the altar linens, the priest's vestments, the gold chalices, the three holy anointing oils, just to name a few.

"As a good Catholic, Gary, do you know the names of the three anointing oils?

"No, I can't say that I do."

"That was one of the first lessons we needed to learn. The first one is named the *Sacrum Chrisma* or sacred chrism. The second oil was called the *Oleum Catechumenorum* or the oil of the catechumens. And the third, which I will never forget, was referred to as *Oleum Infirmorum* or the oil of the infirm and sick.

"There was also a stock of thin hosts, representing the body of Christ. These were given out at communion. But probably best of all was what was stashed in a small refrigerator. It housed the few bottles of wine that were used in the services as a symbol of Christ's blood.

"Being Catholic, or should I say, being forced to be Catholic, while going to the Catholic school, it was a monthly ritual to cross the street with our class to go to the church. We would all sit in a long wooden pew, in silence of course, and wait for a turn to enter the confessional. You know, to meet up with a priest to tell him our sins. It was in the said confessional, mind you that I was forced to go into, that I found myself with the priest in charge of the altar boy training. Let us just refer to him as Father J."

"Is that his full name, just Father J?"

"I mean come on, Gary, you don't want me to do all your hard work, do you? We are going to keep this going for quite some time. No need to give you all the clues right now.

"Did you go to confessional as a child, Gary? How is it that you rid yourself of your wrongdoings these days? Do you still sit, crouching, in front of a Catholic priest asking and begging for forgiveness?"

Not waiting for an answer, Tiberius continues the story. "It was during the altar boy training and these confessionals that Father J groomed me and many other victims. Slowly but surely, this priest would get me to admit my sins and wrongdoings. Even if I did not do anything wrong, he was a master at manipulation and getting you to talk and do things. He would relentlessly tailor me, using guilt as his primary weapon, constantly trying to gain my trust by telling me over and over that he was a friend that I could count on. Through this priming, he ultimately got me to admit that I masturbated, something he considered an unthinkable sin that deserved punishment.

"Ironically, enough, this was the same time in history, that after hundreds of years of traditionally administering Catholic confessionals in separate rooms with a small dark sliding metal grate between the priest and the confessor, that the church wanted to make a change. It was now that the Catholic Church, in all their wisdom, thought it was a good idea to have the option for the confessor to come into the same room as the priest, allowing them to sit face to face with the priest in a closed room, theoretically allowing the confessor to become closer to God in their self-reflection. But really all it did was promote all types of opportunities for grooming and sexual assault to occur at the hands of the priests. It was a decision on the part of the Catholic church that would adversely affect thousands upon thousands of individuals' lives.

"Gary, were you a good little Catholic boy growing up? Being forced to go to confession? I mean let's be honest.

What nine-year-old is going to take it upon himself and say, 'Oh, I better go to church and confess my trivial sins to some priest.' None of us, so let's face it, we were all forced to go. And all the while, you had to admit to some made up tale or fib just to think of something to say when you were in with the priest?"

"Yes, Tiberius, I must admit, I would make up things just to tell the priest. Just like you are referring to."

"Tell me Gary, what god is it that you believe in now? Don't you ever ponder that if there is an all-powerful god, why would you have a job tracking down serial killers? Humph, just food for thought. Let me continue.

"Father J would say how masturbation is a sin. That I would die in hell for doing it. He stated I needed to pray and ask for forgiveness. He'd give me the task of reciting the Hail Mary prayer ten times and the Our Father prayer five times.

"After months of confession, mind you while I was continuing to masturbate because it felt good and that is what boys do, Father J told me I needed more to be cleansed from my sinful disgusting actions. It was then, but only when all the other students had gone back across the street to school, that he made me follow him out of the confessional and into the sacristy, telling my teacher that he had some more altar boy training for me to do.

"It was there in the sacristy that Father J made me expose my penis to him so he could bless it and forgive me for the wrongs and the sins I had so dreadfully committed. As he was standing behind me, Father J reached around me and took my penis in his right hand. He wrapped his middle, ring and pinky fingers around it and tightened his grasp to a firm grip. All the while, his index and thumb stayed pointed outward and relatively straight. This was because of some nerve damage that the priest had in his hand. The priest was unable to bend his index and thumb fingers, making it so that when he grabbed my penis, his index finger pointed to the left, while his nerve damaged thumb followed the direct line of the shaft of my penis while he was holding my organ.

"At first, Father J just held it and started mumbling some sort of prayer or blessing.

Through this holy anointing, may the Lord in His love and mercy help you with the grace of the Holy Spirit, may the Lord who frees you from sin, save you and raise you up my son, this prayer I utter in faith will reclaim you because you are ill, and the Lord will restore you to health, for the sins you have committed, forgiveness will be yours my son.

"I immediately knew this was wrong and tried to escape from the grasp of the priest, but I was told that I would certainly live a short life and die in hell if my demons and the sins that I had committed were not expelled. Father J forcefully held my now ten-year-old body in front of him. I was pressed between the priest and the large antique wooden dresser drawers, the ones that were stained and polished ever so beautifully. After a few minutes of just holding my penis and mumbling those ridiculous prayers, the priest started to move it, slowly but surely making me aroused. Regardless of how much I tried for this not to happen, I quickly had an erection, at which time the priest let go of my penis.

"I briefly sighed some relief, thinking this nightmare was

almost over, but it actually had just begun. It was at this point that the Father opened the drawer that housed the three anointing oils for sacraments. He dipped his repulsive fingers and hand in the *Oleum Infirmorum* or the oil of the infirm or sick. He continued to murmur those prayers as if they meant something while he forcefully held me in place.

"Father J stated clearly that I was a sick boy and I needed to be healed in the eyes of God. Father J, with his oiled-up hand, regained his lame three finger grip on my penis and started to stroke it. Now with the lubrication of the oil, there was no stopping the arousal factor. Even though I was in tears, fearing for my life and completely at the mercy of this sick pervert, Father J masturbated me to full ejaculation, during which time, I could feel the now erect penis of the priest pressing on my back side. As he forced me to stand there in the sacristy of the Catholic church, it was unbeknownst to me that this assault was only the start of forever robbing me of my innocence.

"As my head hung low, I tried to keep my eyes closed, but I was too fearful of what else might happen during the assault. I was forced to look at the hand of this priest. The deformed hand as it was with only the three fingers able to wrap around my penis and his index and thumb still straight because of his lameness. It was this image of his hand, in that configuration, that was eternally burned in my ten-year-old mind.

"I now stood, in silent tears, as I zipped up my pants. This pedophile priest washed his hands in the sink and was drying them on a white linen cloth, the kind with a golden cross lightly embroidered in the corner. Father J started to exclaim with great hope! 'This is the start of your healing my son. God will come to your rescue through me and only me to forgive you of your sins.'"

A long pause ensues. There is only the sound of that long, controlled, and very recognizable exhale of Tiberius' breath as it makes its way out of his lungs into the cool October morning air.

Gary hears an opening and tries to appeal to Tiberius' senses. "Tiberius, that is a tragic story. I am so, so sorry that happened to you. Just because you fell victim to a pedophile in a very unfortunate situation does not mean you have to go on killing people. Why don't you do the right thing? Tell me where you are and I will come and help you. I will make sure you get the help you never received. We will get you better."

Just breathing is audible.

"Fell victim?! Don't patronize me. Don't be so clueless and naïve, Gary. I give you more credit than that.

"Thinking that somehow it was me, that it was I, that did the act of falling to become a victim. Insinuating that it was my fault! And that I was the reason that my ten-year-old body was put in that position. You ask, why not just do the right thing? Well, I did.

"For years, all I did was follow the rules. I was a good boy. I did my homework, got exceptional grades, cleaned my room, did my chores around the house, all without being told or reminded. Even though there were no parents around, I continued to do the right thing. All on my own, I went to swim practice, I went to bed on time, and woke up on my own. I became an altar boy. I learned my prayers and said them every night.

"Where did doing the right thing consistently, over and

over again, ever get me? Well, I just gave you a brief glimpse of where it got me. So much for doing the right things as far as I am concerned. Now, I only do the things I want to do. All in my time, no one else's time.

"Don't give up now, Tiberius. Just because of one person."

"One person? You are aware of the sexual abuse scandal running rampant through the entire Catholic church. From every deacon and want-to-be priest, all the way up to the Pope, the church is corrupt. The Catholic church is a breeding ground for pedophiles. I think you are letting your Catholic upbringing cloud your judgement here, Gary. Let me give you some advice.

"Do not underestimate me, Gary. You will surely pay for it if you do.

"And as far as doing the next right thing? I kind of am. I am taking care of the problem because no one else would."

As the deep breaths again become audible in the otherwise silent darkness on the phone, Gary's face is filled with heart wrenching concern for the actual depth and magnitude of how psychopathic this person is has become very clear in his mind.

Tiberius begins to speak very slowly. "Well Gary, it seems as though I have divulged to you enough information for the time being."

"Tiberius, is that your real name?"

"I would love to continue to chat, but I do believe our time is up for now. I have an appointment in which I need to get to. When we speak again, I hope you are willing to share some insight to your life, maybe some good dialogue on some of those serial killers that you have put away over the years. Yes, it would be interesting to hear how you got so lucky, or perhaps unlucky, in catching some of them. In particular, it would very entertaining to hear your tale on Tristan Colburn. Tristan's story is quite interesting to me.

"Gary, I have been looking forward to playing this game with you for quite a while now. I am glad it has begun."

A blank silence occurs as the phone connection goes dead.

Standing with the October sun warming them in the parking lot of the Parkway Diner, the team stands in shock as they contemplate the story they just heard.

"Tiberius?" Jake says. "Do you really think that is his name?"

"I doubt it. Tiberius was the Roman Emperor beginning in 14 A.D. The Tiberius of ancient times was referred to as one of the gloomiest of men. He was a leader who was described as very dark, reclusive, and somber, as someone who really did not want to be a leader or someone in charge, but circumstances forced him to make a difference.

"No Jake, I am quite certain Tiberius is a self-given name. But we still need to investigate it. Start checking with all the Catholic schools. Start with the ones in New Jersey, Pennsylvania, and New York. See if we can get a hit on a student that was named Tiberius. That is a rather unique name, so maybe we will get lucky. Focus on very affluent towns and suburbs with lots of money. My bet is he was close to New York. He mentioned his father worked long hours in the city.

Stepping back, allowing the conversation to sink in more into his brain, Gary starts to mumble, barely audible at first. "He knows me. Tiberius knows me. How does this guy know so much of my story? He knows I was raised Catholic. He knows I have been working homicide and profiling for a long time. He knows I was the one to catch Tristan Colburn. He knows that Tristan murdered my wife Muriel, even though those police records were never made public.

"I think there is only one way for Tiberius to know that Tristan Colburn killed my wife by savagely slashing her throat only feet from where I stood. Tiberius must have had direct communication with Tristan. Somehow Tiberius and Tristan have had in depth correspondences, possibly just simply through the mail in the disguise of fan letters. A lot of famous killers always attract a large fan base and receive numerous letters from them. I bet Tiberius reached out to Tristan because he was curious about revenge killing. Tristan was one of the most notorious revenge killers in history. It's obvious now that Tiberius kills for revenge just like Tristan did. He kills to somehow make the situation right in his sick mind. Their communications probably started well before his first kill, but their conversations allowed Tiberius to gain knowledge and enough confidence to execute his first kill. It was during these exchanges that Tristan must have told Tiberius the details of how he killed my wife. That would be the only way he could have this information. This is why Tiberius is so connected to me. I guarantee he knew I would be at that World Series game. He wanted me to be the one to try and catch him. It is almost as if Tristan Colburn is still playing with me from behind bars! This is just as much a game for Tristan as it is for Tiberius. Tristan is living vicariously through Tiberius and getting satisfaction out of his kills.

"We need to speak with Tristan. This is definitely a connection we need to probe. Right now, Tristan Colburn is the only person who actually knows who Tiberius is and where he might be. But he is not going to give me any information. I put him away. He is held at the ADX Florence maximum security prison in Colorado, which makes him off limits to almost everyone. We'll need a court order to see him. Ryan, get your FBI higher ups to execute the order for us to gain all-access privilege to Tristan. We need to visit with him and we need to do it now.

"But who? Who would be a good person to send in to interview him? Not a male. I think it needs to be a female. Someone that might be able to get him to open up a bit, to entice him so he is willing enough to give us some insight to his revenge killing. If he has had a connection or has been communicating with Tiberius, this person would need to gain his trust. Enough trust to have him be forthcoming with any information he has on Tiberius. I think they have been in contact somehow. Tristan knows who Tiberius is!"

"What about Christine?" Jake offers up his new colleague.

Gary is intrigued. He looks to his left, where the young, fit, blue eyed, brown haired FBI agent is standing with noticeable anticipation, thinking *yes. Her experience and confidence are strong. She can hold her own. I think over time she could get Tristan to let his guard down and get us the useful information we need.*

"Well, Christine, are you up for it? You will need to get inside the head of Tristan Colburn and earn his trust. Do you think that is something you can do? Tristan is one of the most notorious killers in modern history. He has never even told his side of the story. No one actually knows what happened. We just did our best to piece together the carnage from the gruesome evidence left behind. There were plenty of holes left in our story of what he did that day. It must come under the guise of your research. If he realizes it is because we need him, the table will turn. He will hold all the cards and he won't be as forthcoming."

"Yes! I have been training for an opportunity like this my whole career. My PhD thesis was published on the workings of a serial killer's mind. I can do it. I can and will gain his trust and get him to open up. I agree. I think Tristan, at the very least, has communicated with Tiberius. Although we are not sure how at this point, but he has. That is not as important as getting Tristan to tell us the identity, or possibly the location, of Tiberius. That I can and will do."

"Good, good. This should not take long to set up. The President has classified this case with the highest priority. He deems it as a terrorist attack against the priesthood. He is right. Tiberius has the entire ensemble of priests that make up the Catholic church fearing for their lives. As mentioned, the President has given me full authority in this case. They have given me complete access to the resources of the FBI and US Government to be at our disposal. We need to catch this guy before he kills again.

"Christine and Ryan, pack your bags. You will have wheels up in sixty minutes to head out to Colorado. Once you land, go and get settled. You should hopefully have access to Tristan by tomorrow afternoon."

"Gary, let me have your phone. We need to get the recording of that conversation to the office to be analyzed for speech recognition and patterns. Also, see if there are any background noises that can be identified, especially the music that was playing for the entire conversation. It sounded familiar, but I just could not place it."

"I have that one figured out for you already. It was from the album *The Wall*, by Pink Floyd. I have been listening to that record for over forty years. I know it well. I can place at least two of the song titles that were playing. If my memory serves me correctly, one of the songs was "Goodbye Blue Sky" and the other was "Young Lust." I became too enthralled with the conversation to remember any of the other songs or how many songs played.

"But yes. Get the recording back to forensics. See if they can pick out anything else to help identify Tiberius or his location."

Eleven

Seen through a small six-inch wide window, in front of the over-sized, thick steel plated, reinforced door that leads to the long hallway, Christine takes a few deep breaths to settle her nerves. She waits patiently for the buzzer to sound, which will indicate that she has been cleared to enter. The thick door will open electronically through a computer-authorized mechanism.

Standing tall in modest heels with her black pants fitting snug up her legs, the tightness is outlining her flat stomach and back side. It does not leave much to the imagination. Her white blouse loosely flows over the beauty of her skin as she begins the long walk down the corridor. Her shapely arms are barely covered by the blouse. Her light brown arm hair brushes gently backwards over her rippled forearm as she focuses on the chair that is set out in the distance. There is quite a separation between her and her destination. The impeccably clean, white walkway has only man-made light brightly illuminating the path, for sunlight is almost nonexistent for these types of inmates. The chair is facing the small door of the seven by twelve-foot steel box that Tristan Colburn has resided in since his incarceration.

As the vision of Christine enters the window of Tristan's door, a rush of excitement flows through Tristan as he stands anxiously awaiting his visitor. He is enamored by her glowing beauty and fit body. Taking it all in, he is immediately attracted to her arms and the amount of skin that her blouse is revealing. Although Christine is nervous, she holds herself well. Tristan is a good judge of character and is taken aback by the strength that is obvious in the woman standing in his window.

"Hello, Tristan, I am FBI agent Christine Breeze, based out of the Tampa Bay Federal Offices."

"Of course, welcome!" he says as a smile broadens across his face. "This is such a welcome visit. You have no idea of the amount of joy you have bought into my life by coming to see me. You are a stunning vision that will be held in my mind for eternity. Thank you for coming. I was so excited when I first heard of the visit, I was not even able to eat my lunch." A metal sheet holding mashed potatoes, vegetables and chicken sits untouched off to the side of the dwelling. No utensils are anywhere to be seen.

"Thank you for agreeing to meet with me. This talk will really help with my research."

"Absolutely. However, I could be of service to the fine men and women of FBI."

"I am studying the underlying causes and characteristics of killers. I am looking at all types of killers, ranging from the one-time event killer to the serial killer. I am specifically interested in someone of your type. Someone who has only killed a few times, but who's motivation was seemingly solely based on revenge. I am really trying to identify the motivational aspects that cause a person to go over the edge and take someone's life compared to an average or normal person who would react sanely and figure out how to move on from the situation that gave them so much resentment.

"Can we start with your childhood? What was family life like growing up outside of Chicago?"

"Not so fast, Christine. First, a few things from your end."

Peering through the window, Christine says "Okay, Tristan, you go first."

"Did you shower this morning?"

"Did I shower this morning? Yes, I did shower this morning."

"I can detect the ever so gentle aroma of a lemon ginger fragrance. Was that your standard, run of the mill, Marriott Hotel body wash? Or was that your own body lotion that you bought with you all the way from Tampa Bay?"

"That was my own lotion."

"When you washed in the shower did you shave?"

"Yes, I shaved."

"What did you shave?"

"I shaved my legs and my underarms."

"That is all? Now be honest, Christine."

Pausing, but not breaking eye contact with Tristan. Christine knows how vital these first questions are in order to gain the trust and rapport with Tristan necessary to pursue the information they desire.

"I shaved my pubic hair as well."

"Do you shave it all? Or just part of it?"

"Just part of it."

"Thank you for that. Tell me, after you dried off with the

towel, did you put that special ginger lemon lotion all over your body?"

"Yes, I put it all over my body."

"Where, in particular?"

Knowing what Tristan is wanting, Christine becomes a little flushed in the cheeks. Although feeling her heart rate increase, she holds her professionalism. "Yes, I rubbed it on my arms and across my breasts and nipples."

Tristan's eyes are now piercing through the window at her breasts. Her perfectly shaped, firm breasts lay beautifully behind her blouse, which are only purposely loosely covered. Tristan envies her nipples which are pressing outward on her off-colored white garment.

"What about down there?" Tristan's eyes follow her body down towards the tight outline of her vagina. "Do you rub it where you shaved your pubic hair?"

"Yes, I rub it along the sides of where I shave my pubic hair."

Becoming aroused. Tristan takes a deep breath to savor the moment.

"Thank you, Christine. Speaking of growing up in Chicago, have you ever met an old friend of mine from Chicago Homicide named Gary Hurst?"

"Yes, through my research, I have briefly met Detective Gary Hurst."

"How is my good friend Gary doing? We shared some interesting times together."

"He was doing really well when I had the opportunity to meet him."

"Tell me, Tristan, how is it for you? Eating without any utensils for the last twenty-five years?"

"Ah, touché Christine." Tristan is feeling respect and admiration for the agent. "Very witty of you to notice. Well, I get by. It makes eating interesting to say the least."

"Since you mentioned Gary, why don't you tell me a little about yourself? Why don't you tell me about the fateful incident that has landed you in the highest security prison in the world for the rest of your life?"

"Well, I do have some time on my hands. I do not seem to be going anywhere, now do I?"

"To show you how much I have appreciated our exchange up to this point, I will tell you my story. The story that only one other living person really knows. Honestly, it did not take that long to plan. It all just kind of came to me. You see, it's easy to manipulate people. All you need to do is just take a little time to study their behavior.

"Jimmy Knotzo drove his red Cadillac out of his three-car garage religiously every morning at five minutes after seven. Having taken the time on my part to notice this behavior, Jimmy made it very easy for me to have undetected entry into his rather large house.

"It was one of those sunny spring mornings. The light glistened off the dew on the green grass as I waited under the hedges right next to the garage. The flowers were just budding their spring colors through the gardens in the neighborhood.

"I needed to wait for the perfect moment. He always checked in his rear-view mirror to make sure the garage was closing after he pushed the button while he was turning out of the driveway. He always took a final glance when the door was about half way down. I timed it perfectly as I rolled out from the hedges and right under the closing garage door. I cleared it with about eight inches to spare. It was a seamless entry for me into his house.

"I found myself, safely undetected, inside the dark silent garage of my former boss. Only his wife was home in the kitchen as she enjoyed her eggs and morning television show. She would be easy prey, for I knew his twenty-year-old daughter would not be home from the local college campus until after her last class at 2 o'clock.

"I quietly prepared in the garage. In the darkness, slowly unzipping my backpack, I removed one of the many rolls of duct tape. Leaving my backpack, I proceeded to attend to the task at hand. I made my way over to the door that led directly into the kitchen, which was bright from the morning sun. There was a large bank of windows facing the seemingly endless forest of trees in their back yard. I opened the door undetected because of the volume of her television show. I crept up slowly behind her and I forcefully pushed her off the chair and planted her on the hard-cold marble floor. I squarely drove my knee into the center of her back to hold her in place. I quickly grabbed her arms and secured them behind her back with the duct tape. I caught her by such surprise that the shock in itself subdued her quite a bit. It was quick with not much of a fight on her part. Before she could gather her senses and scream, I taped her mouth shut, although because of the large two-acre lots that these houses had in this neighborhood, no one would have heard her pleas for help anyway.

"I pulled her upright with force as the fear in her eyes became real. Looking at mine, she recognized me immediately, for it was in this same kitchen that I had attended multiple holiday and department gatherings when I worked for Jimmy Knotzo.

"She was dressed only in her silk robe, underwear, and bra. Taking her by the arm, I aggressively moved her through the kitchen to the basement door. I led her down the stairs to what Jimmy referred to as his man cave. A rather large finished basement, this man cave of his housed a wet bar, three large screen TV's, a pool table, a ping pong table, and plenty of chairs and couches.

"Having been a very mediocre athlete without much success, Jimmy Knotzo turned into an avid sports fan and liked to watch multiple games at the same time on all his TVs. This somehow was one of the many ways he boosted his unfounded ego.

"I taped her ankles together. Kneeling her like a dog, I briefly undid the tape around her wrists, only to then outstretch her arms around one of the cement foundational poles commonly found in basements and secured her to that. As the tears flowed in fear down her face, she had no idea how tragically disturbing her day was going to turn out.

"It was around two forty-five that Paisley, Jimmy's twenty-year-old daughter, made her way through the kitchen door, shouting "Mom, Mom" two times before I grabbed her from behind. I covered her mouth and choked her until she fell unconscious. The cute, usually perky blond was rendered helpless. It made it rather easy to transport her down the stairs and tape her up. I securely connected her to the pool table. She was not going anywhere.

"I was almost caught off guard when I heard the garage door opening at four thirty, for Jimmy usually did not arrive home until after five. But since this was his last day of work before they were leaving on a family road trip the next morning, he cut out of the office a little bit early.

"I quickly positioned myself behind the door, preparing myself for more of a struggle, for my first two victims were subdued rather easily. By this time, I had retrieved my backpack from the garage and had the heavy wooden-handled gun in my hand. As Jimmy walked through the door, with his stupid, goofy, shit-eating grin on his face, with the butt of my gun I pegged him right on the bridge of his nose, just about shattering his nose. I busted his wire rimmed glasses and immediately put him on his backside, out cold. As he lay there, the blood exploded from what was once his nose onto his 300-dollar custom white shirt.

"With his wife duct taped to the pole and the daughter secured to the pool table, I set Jimmy right in his favorite leather wooden chair. Using an abundant amount of tape, I secured his ankles, legs, chest, arms, and wrists tightly to the heavy piece of furniture. His head was drooping forward as his face slowly dripped blood onto his no longer white shirt. The two women in his life sobbed silently in desperation. His wife was off to his left and his daughter was off to the right. There was a big space between the three of them as he faced the large wall housing all his TVs.

"Slapping his face back and forth, it took a while, but I was able to bring Jimmy back to his painful reality, a reality that he would forever regret because of his past actions. He gargled his own blood as he realized he could not breath through his nose anymore. Catching somewhat of a breath, it was his wife that first came into focus. Then as he saw his daughter, he immediately started to squirm. Nothing moved. Not the chair, not him, nothing.

"As I stood in front him, his eyes focused on my face. 'Hello, Jimmy. Remember me?' Shaking his head yes, some tears started to roll down his bloody face. 'Good. I wasn't sure if you would. It has been five years since you fired me.'"

"What do you want?"

"All in due time, Jimmy. Don't worry, this could all turn out fine for you and your lovely blond-haired daughter and wife. It really all depends on you. But isn't that how you like it anyway? Being the big man in charge, calling all the shots, making things happen. Making decisions that severely affect people's lives. Isn't that why they pay you the big bucks?

"Let me just catch you up on my life after you fired me and blacklisted me from getting another job in the only industry I knew. You fired me mainly because I called you out on the sexual discrimination you continually exhibited when I was in the process of hiring the best sales team in the country. You would always make me hire much less qualified and less experienced women because you thought I needed more females on my team. But of course, all the females you made me hire were younger and very attractive.

"After I reported you to human resources to hold you accountable for your actions, you immediately started pulling all my resources. You started negating all the contractual promises you had made to me upon my hiring, the promises that you said would be in place for me to build the department that I would lead. You made us get by on scraps for resources, putting me and my team at a complete disadvantage with our competitors and within the rest of our own company. Quite frankly, it was only through work ethic and determination that while working under complete adverse conditions that my team was as successful as it was.

"After two years of excelling with what we had, regardless of the limitations you had put on me, my team still only met average numbers within the industry, and then you fired me, stating performance issues as the reason.

"We both know that is not true. You just could not handle someone in your ranks standing up to you and telling you what being business smart and morally right actually was. Telling you what was better for the company other than hiring the next attractive woman that came through the door. I was unlike the rest of the puppets you had working for you. I had a backbone. I had the conviction to stand up for people's rights. You were so dismayed by my actions to hold you liable that you set a plan in action to let me go.

"I also know you blacklisted me. Other CEO's would tell me exactly that, off the record of course, but they would not hire me because of you. It was only after a short two years of unemployment that we lost our house and were on food stamps to feed my family. It was around this time that my wife and youngest son were tragically both killed by a drunk driver.

"Trying to show some sympathy. Jimmy said, 'Oh my gosh,

I am so sorry. Let me give you a job…let me give you a recommendation. I can fix this.' He cried as he pleaded in desperation.

"Too late for any of that, Jimmy. It was about six months after the death of my wife and son that my older son took his own life. He mentioned you in his suicide note, stating that ever since you fired me from my job his life had taken such a drastic turn for the worse, that it just wasn't worth living anymore.

"Hearing the truth and repercussions of Jimmy's actions for the first time, his daughter and wife are bawling, weeping in sorrow about my family that they once knew.

"All I want is some truth, Jimmy. Admit what you did. Admit that you took away my resources. Admit that you lied. Admit why you fired me, blacklisted me, and ruined my life. Admit that you are the root cause of the death of my wife and two kids. If you do this and follow some simple directions, you will all live.

"Okay, Okay, Okay." With his now disfigured and bloodied face, Jimmy tried to start to explain. "It is true, I admit it. You were a diamond in the rough. Someone that could probably take over my job. I feared how good you were. Then once you called me out for my gender discrimination, I knew I had to get rid of you. I pulled all the resources I had promised you. I lied to you. I said I would give you those things and I didn't. I was in fear of your success and how it would overshadow me. My ego was too big, and I had to use my power to keep you at bay and get rid of you. I knew I needed to blacklist you. You were too good. In fact, you were exceptional. If you got a job at one of my competitors, you would immediately start to take over the industry."

"Good, good. That is refreshing to finally hear you admit it. Tell me more. Why else did you fear me? I know there must have been more.

"Walking over and grabbing her long blond hair, jerking her head back, I exposed his daughter's flushed red face covered in snot and tears: 'Your vibrant young daughter's life depends on it.'

"Okay, please not her. I will tell you, I will tell you. It was before you even went to human resources. It was that one department staff meeting that I was introducing one of our new sales directors to the company. It was Brenda Nails."

"Yes, I remember her. I remember her because she was young and inexperienced, but very attractive. Kind of like your daughter here. I remember her getting the job over many other well-qualified men and women."

"Yes, that's her. I admit that I hired her solely because I was attracted to her and wanted to sleep with her," said Jimmy as his wife sobbed in disgust.

"If you recall, I always arrived a little late to the staff meetings, especially when I was introducing a new employee. I liked walking down the long open stairway that would open directly into the large open room. It stroked my ego, walking down the stairs, looking down upon all my people as if I were their king. Yes, I know it is sick thinking. I am trying to be honest to save my family."

"This is good, please continue."

"Well, if you recall that meeting when I was introducing

Brenda Nails, you arrived a few steps behind us, following us down the stairs. When I stopped about ten steps from the bottom to address my people and look down upon them as I introduced this new employee, you happened to be about three stairs behind us. You had no choice but to stop in your tracks. You stood there patiently, not bothering anyone. No one except for me that is.

"For having you above me on the stairs, as I looked down upon my kingdom, was unacceptable. How dare you take your place on the stairs perched higher than I, towering over me as I presented myself. I knew at that moment that I would be firing you somehow. My ego could not take that."

"Wow! You are sicker than I even thought. To destroy a man's life, solely based on your unwarranted ego and self-image! Absolutely disgusting. You are an embarrassment to mankind."

"Yes, yes, I know. I am a disgrace. I admit I lied to you. I ruined your life."

"A little late for self-reflection, don't you think, Jimmy?" I said as I swayed back and forth, slowly contemplating the moment. "This is what we are going to do now. Do you want to live, Jimmy?"

"Yes, yes, yes!" There was a glimmer of hope heard in his answer.

"Do you want to save the lives of your beautiful daughter and your most attractive wife? Do you Jimmy?"

"Yes, yes, please, I beg you. What do I have to say? What do I have to do to fix this?"

I stood with my gun in hand, pacing in a triangular path,

making my way from the daughter to the wife then to back to Jimmy. I repeated the pacing pattern, gently tapping each one with the silver barrel of the gun. Sometimes I would even just caress it over their skin.

"This is what you are going to do.

"Grabbing a black handled, shiny eight-inch hunting knife out of my backpack, I told Jimmy, 'I am going to free your daughter from the pool table.' I walked over and cut the tape off her wrists. I saw relief in the eyes of the three victims. Paisley was still bound at her ankles and her knees. I guided her to then crawl her way over to Jimmy and kneel in front of him.

"Paisley knelt in front of her dad with a straight back. Her hands were at her side and her long blond hair was disheveled from the day's events. She stared into her father's eyes, with a silent stare, pleading in desperation for her father to somehow help her..."

Over the next few minutes, Tristan described in vivid and excruciating detail what he forced Paisley and Jimmy to do. As Christine listened to the story and having had previous knowledge of what the forensics team found at the crime scene, the vision of the actual events now played out in the forefront of Christine's mind. The disturbing images sped through her consciousness like a runaway freight train screaming endlessly through the darkness of the night with no way of stopping it in sight. Christine worked hard to stay calm and not show the total revulsion she felt sweep over her as she heard the story being narrated to her firsthand from the voice of the killer. The most horrid she has ever heard in her life, which included Tristan's over the top description of how he slit Paisley's throat to end her life. She tuned back in as Tristan raised his voice to end that part of the story with, "I turned my head to the right, in the direction of where Jimmy sat. I looked at him directly and said. 'OH! I lied as well! I lied too, Jimmy,' almost shouting with honor. 'How about that? What do you think about that? Any good words of wisdom you would like to share now?'"

Pulling himself out of his storytelling daze, Tristan peers his eyes back through the window at Agent Christine. Noticing the sweat dripping from under her arms, he caught her right as she was about to throw up from her disgust at what she'd just heard. It was only a slight gag as she quickly regained her composure.

"Tristan, it is a good thing that you are on the other side of that steel door."

"Oh, please, Christine. Spare me. If you are up for it, I will finish my tale."

Swallowing her saliva, she says, "Please continue."

"I did not do anything for a while after that. I just walked around the basement a bit, letting the event sink into Jimmy's mind to have the most impact as possible. I reveled in the revenge I had taken on him.

"Please kill me, kill me now," Jimmy was mumbling as he was finally able to speak some minutes later.

"No, sorry my friend. That would be too easy for you.

"I sliced through the tape that was holding his wife to the pole. She was barely more than a rag doll at this point due to the shock of the day. But she was still very aware of her surroundings. I removed her skimpy underwear and bra. With my bloody blade pressing against the skin of her hip, I walked her across the room. I bent her over at the waist and leaned her forward to rest her arms and head on the shoulders of her husband.

Agent Christine listened with more absolute disgust as Tristan described the raping and then the swift killing of Jimmy's wife right in front of him. The horror of these images seeped deep down into Agent Christine's bones, forever disturbing her soul with Tristan's depiction of the day's events. Tristan finished with, "This was the scene that I left. Jimmy alive, unable to move as he was strapped in his big leather chair, with his dead wife bleeding out all over him and his daughter dead at his feet.

"Ah yes! I almost forgot to tell you one of the pure beauties of the day. Earlier Jimmy had mentioned that he thought he saw something in his rear-view mirror. Something slipping under his garage door. He figured that couldn't be anything and didn't think twice. He didn't turn around to check. For if he had, this whole day most likely would have been thwarted.

"This next part was an absolutely genius, a part of the plan. Since they were going on a three-day road trip to visit his brother in Arizona, no one even noticed they were missing for days. It wasn't until they did not show up in Arizona and the brother could not reach them on their cell phones that he called the police. It was four days before they were even found.

"I must say, it was brilliant planning it for the eve of their vacation, knowing they would not be noticed missing for days. Jimmy Knotzo was living in the abyss between life and death for days, being tortured with the reality that laid before him. That little fact right there might be what I value and honor most about what happened.

"When they found them, Jimmy was almost dead from dehydration, starvation, and probably shock. But he lived. Thankfully.

"Tell me Christine, how is my good friend Jimmy Knotzo doing these days?"

"He is doing very well. That was twenty-five years ago and he has a whole different life now with a whole different family," Christine lied right through the dryness of her almost oversized lips. She was well aware that Jimmy Knotzo is being housed in a psychiatric ward in upstate New York. Jimmy Knotzo had never uttered a word since he was found. She was not going to give Tristan the satisfaction of knowing this.

"Well, it can't be that good. I know I must haunt his every waking moment."

"I will admit, Tristan, that was a chilling story," she says, giving Tristan a little of what he wanted and a little satisfaction. "But tell me. You have had years stacked upon years of self-reflection. Do you have regrets? Are you ever sorry for what you did?"

"Interestingly enough, as tragic as it was, I still sometimes ponder a question to this day. Was it an equal trade of misery? Most of the time I believe it was. And maybe even a little more so. I think yes, I won. I do not doubt that I inflicted way more misery on him than he did on me. I am convinced of that fact. I believe the life of my wife and the lives of my two children were worth it. That being said, I would do it again. I have no regrets. The memories of that day are a part of what keep me going every day. In my mind, I revel in the victory day in and day out."

"That is very interesting, Tristan. It sounds like you are quite proud of the revenge you took upon Jimmy. In all my years, I have never heard anything like that. It is extremely sad and disheartening to know that people like you exist. But at the same time, it reassures me that my work and research is important. Your story will be very helpful to me. Thank you for sharing."

"You say you are from the Tampa Bay FBI Office. Any chance you were working on the World Series murder? Yep, I know about that. I thought it was great. Get this, the warden thought it would be a good idea to allow the inmates, most of us killers, to watch the World Series in the confines of our own isolation. Then one of the greatest murders put on the world stage was pumped right into our cells."

"No, not really. Only peripherally," Christine says, trying not to let Tristan have too much information. "I only did some back up interviews for a few days and then I was told to get back to my research. Why do you ask, Tristan? What do you think about it? Does your experience give you any insight to who or what type of man this is?"

Wanting to build and keep his relationship with his new-found attractive visitor, Tristan continues the conversation. "I have been thinking a lot about him. I think he is after revenge. Not unlike what motivated me. Tell me, Christine. Has he killed again? We are only exposed to edited news. Only soft news. Nothing hard or violent."

Christine lies again. "No, not that we know of."

"Well, I bet it was not his first kill. Way too elaborate of a plan. It would have been very daring for his first killing to be in such a public setting. If you are asking for my advice, I would look for some type of killing from the past to match his M.O. Something with a similar signature. This was too great of a scheme for him to stop now. I am almost sure he will be doing it again and again. He probably won't stop until he is put away or killed. At least that is what I think. Once you start killing, you get a liking to it. I certainly did."

"Tristan, you are allowed to have correspondences with your hundreds and hundreds of sick fans?"

"Yes, yes, I am."

"Do you think this killer may have ever reached out to you?"

"Well, maybe," smirking as he turns his head to the side, trying unsuccessfully to hide his smile.

Christine knows at this moment that he has been in contact with their killer. Tactfully moving forward as not to show any signs of excitement, she says "Interesting. Can you tell me anything about him?"

"Maybe. What are you going to do for me? If I do, will you be sure to come back and visit me for more research?"

"Yes, I will do that. I will come back and visit with you."

"It sure would be nice to eat some meals with utensils again. Do you think you could use your persuasiveness with the warden to reinstate my utensil privileges?"

"I will promise you this. I will do my best."

As a slight smile broadens on Tristan's face. "All I will tell you is that you are dealing with a very fierce and driven individual. A northerner at that."

Simultaneously, the buzzer sounds and the clank of the steal door far down the hallway starts to open.

"Sounds like our time is up, Christine."

"Wait! What do you mean by a northerner?"

"Let's save that for next time. It was an absolute pleasure visiting with you. Your beauty and your lemon ginger scent will stay with me always."

As the guards arrive at Christine's side, they escort her out of the lockdown area.

Twelve

With three days' worth of facial growth, Jake sips his black coffee at his desk. He is working at his computer setting up the day's route to hit a list of more churches. It has been weeks of just canvassing all the Catholic churches, talking to any residing priests and trying to track down any adults that were former altar boys that might possibly resemble the killer. There are teams investigating in every conceivable northern part of whatever and wherever. Going off what Tristan mentioned, they are feverishly tracking almost every northern part of anything. North Philly, northern Maryland, northern New York State and City, and of course Gary's team is still focused right here in northern New Jersey. What Tristan meant by *he is a northerner* is unknown. It could have meant so many things. But until they know better, the focus is on the churches in the northern areas of these states. Regardless of the number, this is the prime course of action.

There's been no word from Tiberius during this time. He could just be laying low, planning his next kill. All of the ways that Tristan could possibly communicate out to Tiberius have been shut down so that there could be no warning given to him.

"Christine! Have you found anything from that stack of cold cases you've been going through?"

"No, Jake, not yet. This is tedious work. I have only made my way through about half of them. Ryan and I have two unis helping me as well. But we haven't found anything yet. We all spend a few hours on this every morning before we head out to the churches on our list for the day. Then I spend a few more hours at night when I get back."

Gary comes walking through the doors to the office. Passing Christine, he pauses at her desk. "Christine, I just want to reiterate again how good of a job you did with interviewing Colburn. You got him to trust you and talk about things he has never shared with anyone. You got him to give us some crucial information on Tiberius which I know will help us catch him. You also uncovered vital information from the decades old case, and finally helped us piece together what actually happened in the Knotzo murders. That information will be studied and used in profiling for generations to come.

"Thank you, Gary. That means a lot to me. Now let's get this sicko before he kills again."

"I am right with you on that, Christine!"

"Jake, you about ready to go? We got a lot of road time ahead of us today. I want to get to it."

Heading out to the car, Gary says, "Hey! I stopped and got us a few Taylor ham, egg, and cheese on a hard roll."

"With Sal-Pep-Ketch?" Jake smirks.

"Yes, of course. Is there any other way!"

Gary and Jake make their way, driving through the small towns in Passaic County. They head to the location of their second church of the day. "You know, Gary, I will admit, these breakfast sandwiches are not half bad. They might not be the healthiest thing for you, but they are pretty satisfying and filling."

"I told you! I am glad you are becoming a little more open minded."

Gary starts to steer the conversation to Tiberius. "I agree with what Colburn said about Tiberius. He is fierce. The worst kind of fierce, because he is being driven by vengeance. We know from our last conversation that he has issues with Catholic priests and the church. This really doesn't help us, given that his next victim could be any one of the near forty thousand Catholic priests still left in America. The victim could be from any state. For all we know, Tiberius could be in California right now, studying and planning with extraordinary detail how death will befall the next unsuspecting priest. He is playing a very strategic game. He is intelligent and he is motivated. We know he is not going to stop. It will happen again.

Jake starts to add to his list. "At least we know he is targeting priests. We need to somehow find out who this Father J is or was. If we can pinpoint him, we can then identify all the altar boys that were serving in his parish or parishes. That would help narrow our focus. That is also assuming that Tiberius is in the same location where all the abuse occurred when he was younger. That is one long, thin line to follow to catch our guy."

Silence overtakes the drive as the car passes by the now naked branches of the tree-lined street. They are in a picturesque, quaint town of blue-collar workers. As they sit at a red light, Gary's phone rings. They both look at each other as they see it is from an unknown caller. Taking a deep breath, Gary swipes the phone to answer.

"Hello, this is Gary."

"Gary." The depth of Tiberius' voice bellows through the phone. "This is your friend calling."

"Is this Tiberius?"

"Yes."

"Good to hear from you, Tiberius. I haven't heard from you in a while. It's been quiet from your end. What have you been doing?"

"I have been busy. I am always busy, Gary. I always have things to do. Things to plan."

"Plan? What are you planning?"

"Isn't that what you and your partner should be figuring out? Gary, I think by now you should know a little bit more about how our game is being played. I do things. I plan things. I bring death to those individuals who have earned such a demise. I am taking care of business and doing a great service to this world. All while you try and catch me."

"Tiberius, you don't have to do this so-called service to the world. I know you had issues as a child with the church. But why don't you just let us help you? Things are different now. Tell us who hurt you and let the Justice Department do their thing. They will investigate and arrest anyone that did anything wrong. I promise. I know you were abused, but all this killing can stop now, and we can help you before it gets any worse."

Speaking slowly and sporadically through his deep breaths, Tiberius says "It seems to be only getting worse for the people who deserve it. I am not too concerned about it. I am certainly not too concerned about getting caught by you. You aren't even close."

"Why don't you tell me more about yourself? As unsettling as it was, I was happy to listen to the story you told us last time. Why not elaborate on that?" Gary starts just driving endlessly around the small town as the conversation continues.

"Tell me, Gary. Did you pray this morning? Did you pray before that ever precious first cup of coffee that I know you detectives rely so heavily on?"

"Yes, I did. I prayed first thing."

"Do you pray on your knees?"

"Yes. I pray on my knees."

"Directly on the floor? Or do you put something between your old knobby knees and the floor?"

"I put a small pillow down for cushion."

"You know, Gary. I think I have you figured out pretty well. You think you are a good Catholic, praying to God and probably making your requests all while you praise Jesus, the supposed son of God, who died for you. But you can't even find it deep inside of yourself to sacrifice a little bit and kneel directly on the floor because it is a bit uncomfortable! What's the matter, Gary? Wasn't his sacrifice of his own life worthy enough for you to just get on your knees? After all the years you have spent on this earth, you still pray as if it actually works. Tell me, what did you pray for this morning?"

"I prayed the Our Father and Hail Mary. I asked God for enduring strength. I thanked God for his grace. I asked to be able to do my job and catch you before you kill again."

"God's grace? So, are you living in God's grace, Gary?"

"Yes, I believe I am."

"So, tell me, Gary, why do you think God sheds his grace on you and not on others? You really can't be that naïve. Do you really believe this God of yours is somewhere picking and choosing who he is going to allow to live in his grace? Where was this so-called grace of God on September eleventh? Where was this grace when so many people in this world needed it?"

"The grace of God is there. It is real. You have to be willing to believe. You have to be aware of your surroundings and what is going on in your life. You must be grateful for what you have in this life. Then you will start to realize that the grace of God has been right with you your entire life."

"My experience leads me to believe different. It is obvious to me that this prayer thing is not working out for you. Why do you still you do it? Don't you ever ask yourself why?"

"Only on occasion do I doubt my convictions. I think it is only human. But I always come back to my faith stronger than ever. It's what I do. It's how I get through each day. So I must vehemently disagree, Tiberius. I believe it is working."

"Ah, well thank you for your insight, however, misguided it may be."

"Quid pro quo, Tiberius. Tell me some more about yourself."

"Well, I do think most of my planning is done for the day. I have some time and I think it will make our game a little more intriguing. So, why not?"

Silence ensues as Tiberius pauses for a while. Gary only knows Tiberius is still there because his deep breaths are audible.

Then Tiberius begins. "It was a chilly October day and Tiberius was sitting in his 5th grade math class. 'BING, BING, BONG,' the PA speaker sounded, giving its usual alert when the principal had an announcement. 'Miss Crabtree,' said the old frail voice which came through the worn cracked old speaker hanging in the corner of the room, 'could you please send Tiberius over to the church? He has been requested to be an altar boy for a funeral being served by Monsignor Hooten.'

"Relief came over Tiberius. At least it wasn't with that bastard Father J, who had continually assaulted him over the past year. Tiberius had managed to steer clear of the molesting priest for the past four months. Tiberius was now eleven years old and with the start of the new school year, he was starting to gain his confidence back and was becoming himself again.

"After all, so what if some pervert priest grabbed my dick and jerked it a few times. I was better than letting that get the best of me. I was not going to let some sick man get to me and hold me back or keep me down. I figured no big deal, time to move on with a new beginning. I had not seen him in over four months. Out of sight and out of mind."

"So, was this your turning point?"

"Well…I guess you could say that. But for now, let me continue.

"The colored leaves of the fall drifted down to their resting place on the manicured green grass and the grey-black asphalt of the street. Wearing my light fall jacket, I made my way through the white-lined crosswalk. The chill of a soft October breeze brushed up my back, the sort of breeze that is only recognizable through the innocence of a carefree child. At this moment, I had the feeling that anything, absolutely anything, in this life was possible. It was this feeling that gave me a little extra lift in my step as I crossed the street heading into the rectory to be of service to what I thought was my God.

"As I entered the silence of the rectory, realizing nobody was around, I made my way down the long dimly lit hallways. There was the occasional depressing picture hanging on the wall of some old person that was supposed to be a saint or of such similar status in the Catholic church. Passing the occasional closed wooden door, I nonchalantly walked down the ugly greenish carpeting, sporadically passing more pictures, I turned right down a hallway that had a few folding chairs leaning against the walls. This final turn led me into the sacristy.

"Feeling good and upbeat, I started setting the altar for the funeral as I retrieved Monsignor Hooten's golden chalice from the antique cabinet. Every priest has his own personally designed gold chalice. They are very expensive and are under lock and key in a particular drawer. The combination was etched in pencil on the side of another unlocked wooden drawer. The location is only known by the priests and some select few altar boys. The altar boys that know the combination are given this secret hiding place during the grooming process. The divulgence of this so-called valuable secret is used by the priests to gain the altar boy's trust. This trust is used in the process to later ultimately sexually assault the boys. So yes, I had the knowledge of the secret hiding place of the combination to unlock the chalices.

At first, it was hard to remember which chalice belonged to which priest. God forbid if you set out the wrong chalice for the wrong priest, you would get a lashing with the leather belt. But after three years of being an altar boy, I had them all memorized. Monsignor Hooten's had a particularly vibrant red ruby displayed in the base of his, while Father Fishtone's had his mother's wedding ring securely attached to the underside bottom of his chalice. The unmentionable Father J had a diamond right smack in the middle of the cup. It seemed that when he would show it off, it boosted his unfounded ego, somehow implying that he was as all powerful and indestructible as the diamond.

"There were very few things that an altar boy looked forward to doing. In fact, I am not even sure if any altar boy actually liked being an altar boy. They are usually forced by their parents to start doing it. And of course, after the grooming and the sexual assaults, you definitely do not like anything to do with being an altar boy, the church, or God for that matter.

"But before the sexual assaults started, it was always fun to sneak a little wine before and after serving a mass, wedding or funeral. It was a common practice that I took part in and rather enjoyed. It was also nice after a funeral or wedding, for you usually got kicked two or three bucks by the funeral or wedding director.

"And of course, there was the lighting of the incense. The incense came in these oval shaped charcoal briquettes. You were only supposed to use one, but I always used two to enhance the fragrance and the smoke. The briquettes were placed in a golden censer. The censer is similar to a cauldron with unique designs and openings to allow for the smell and the smoke to disperse into the room while the incense is burning. It was carried by a long chain that the priest held as he swung the canister from side to side and up and down in the formation of a cross. The fragrance is very unique, and I have never smelled anything else like it. As a young kid, this aroma is impressionable and stays with you forever. It was kind of fun, for once you lit the briquette, it caught fire on one side and the fire spread rapidly like a firecracker fuse would as it engulfed the entire briquette.

"The funeral went off without a hitch. The fragrance and the smokiness of the incense seemed extra strong in the sacristy when I went to retrieve it for the appropriate moment during the service. Smelling and making my way through the thick smoke in sacristy always gave me a short lived internal little smirk of joy.

"At the end of the funeral, the director came in and handed me three dollars. This was great, because as an eleven-year old it is hard to come by any money unless you are lifting it out of dad's wallet. Monsignor Hooten had quickly vanished from the sacristy after the funeral, mumbling something about a lunch meeting he had in town at noon. As the casket, being carried by six faithful family members, floated its way down the front granite stairs of the church, I found myself all alone cleaning up the sacristy. I folded the linens, hung the Monsignor's vestment back in the closet, cleaned out his golden ruby encrusted chalice and locked it back up in the drawer. Stepping outside to dump and extinguish the still burning incense briquettes from the censer, the coldness of the mid-morning made its way to my bones.

"'Doing the next right thing'…as you would say, right, Gary."

Gary just gulps and encourages Tiberius to continue, not wanting to interrupt his flow.

"Upon entry back into the sacristy, I found myself no longer alone. Fear gripped me as Father J stood at the opposing doorway tapping his foot, glaring his disgusting eyes down at me. 'Avoiding me it seems, have you?' exclaimed the pedophile.

"Scared out of my wits, every ounce of confidence that I had gained back over the last four months was now rushing out of my soul at a million miles an hour. Almost all of it was to be drained from me with in seconds of sighting this monster.

"'Uh, uh,' I stumbled over my words, 'nnnn…nnnnn…no, I have not, I have just been busy' I exclaimed with a dry mouth, feeling as dehydrated as Death Valley in California would be in mid-August.

"In a last-ditch effort for survival, I turned in an attempt to run and exit through the two doors that led to the outside and to my freedom. It was here, in my haste, that I banged my head on the large wooden center piece where the two large doors came together to close, becoming slightly dazed from the violent collision of running for my life at full speed into the solid piece of wood.

"It was this moment, which was the smallest moment in time, that would forever change everything in my life. For it was this miniscule moment when I was dazed that gave Father

J the opportunity to rush forward and grab me by the collar. He hoisted me backwards with what seemed like the force of ten men. The displacement of my body was so violent that it landed me directly front and center of an all too unfortunate and familiar place right at the mid-point of the large wooden antique counter of cabinets and drawers. With this type of effort and violence being thrust upon me, I knew then that the outcome of what was about to occur was not going to be good. Father J was vengeful towards me for avoiding him and I was about to feel his wrath.

"With my head still pounding, the hands of the priest quickly undid my belt, pants button, and zipper. He forcefully seized my penis with his traditional three finger grip. This instantly removing any thoughts of head pain that I had seconds ago from running into the center piece of the door. Unfortunately, the priest's displeasure in my sneaking around to avoid him and my failed attempt at escape him only moments before had made him take this assault to another level. Now with my pants down around my knees, he forcefully and violently stroked and masturbated me to erection with all my attempts to stop this from happening failing.

"There was no God in my life. There was no savior that was going to come save me. In the depths of the sacristy, as my own father would say, of the all holy and all good Catholic church, I had again found myself at the mercy of this man, if you want to refer to him as that. A man that would sexually assault me and take from me any shred of decency and innocence that I had left. I was alone, more alone than any person would ever feel. I was the loneliest person in the history of humankind. I was doomed at the hands of this monster. It would be for his sick pleasure, and my most certain demise, that the impending and most catastrophic change of a life course ever thought possible was about to be delivered by him and only him.

"Making his move for the oil in the drawer, I thought yes, this is my chance to make a break for it. I elbowed him with all the might in my eleven-year-old body, only to be pushed back. He thrust me forward into the cabinets with such a driving force that my still erect penis and testicles slammed into the wood, creating such an acute, sharp pain that I almost passed out. But this was not the most severe pain I was going to feel today. Despite the loneliness and desperation that I had already embarked upon, I did not think it could get any worse. But yes, much more was to be revealed.

"As the sacristy was still redolent with smoke from the incense that had burned for almost two hours, it was now that so many things happened almost simultaneously. The priest had oiled both of his hands, and while his right hand with his bum index and thumb digits had aggressively started masturbating me again his left hand, now oiled up, was stroking his own penis. Almost unbeknownst to me, while I was in the midst of being slammed into the cabinet and he was reaching for the oil, he also managed to drop his own pants. Within what seemed like nanoseconds, he had thrust his cock so far up my ass I thought it was going to come out right through my eyes. Any oil he might have had on his penis did nothing to soothe the violent entry of him impaling me, causing me the greatest physical pain and mental anguish I had ever known. To this day, I have never experienced anything like it.

"Gary, you asked about my turning point. Well perhaps…right there, right then…that was my moment. The moment of my incomprehensible demoralization. The instant that was the real turning point in my life.

"As he penetrated me deeply, it gave me no choice but to glare upward. Gazing up above the cabinets at the off white, very drably painted wall, I found myself staring at a cross. The image of this twenty-one-inch metallic cross pierced down through my sky-blue eyes, penetrating deep into my soul. This vision became embedded unfathomably within me, as if this cross was being heated to a molten white orange color to be branded into my memory forever to live. To live in this life and the life hereafter. That is if there is a life hereafter.

"While thrusting and driving himself into me, he continued to stroke my penis. He was gripping me so fiercely with his left hand that his unmanicured fingertips were digging deeply into my left shoulder, drawing blood. Now with the smoke irritating my eyes and the scent of the incense penetrating my senses, it made this moment in time like nothing else. But it was at this point that I heard someone enter the sacristy.

"With silent tears running down my cheeks, my shoulder bleeding from his fingernails and my ass oozing blood because he had torn me wide open with his raping of my body and my soul, the young Deacon Eric stood at the doorway in disbelief. He stood with his tanned skin and blondish, sun-bleached hair, for he had just returned from a trip down in South America. And I thought, *Yes, I am saved. There is a GOD, he did not leave me to die, with nothing, in my most dire of circumstances.*

But nothing stopped.

The forceful grip on my shoulder holding me in place did not ease up. The voracious pounding on my now more bloodied ass seemed to be increasing with his pleasure of knowing we were possibly caught, all while my penis was now in the tightest three finger grip ever conceivable.

"Eric!" Exclaimed Father J. "Just turn around and leave…leave like nothing ever happened or the ordaining of your priesthood that you have been so feverishly working towards over the past eight years will never ever occur."

"But Father J, what is going on? This can't be right," replied the confused deacon.

"Deacon Eric," the priest shouted with everything he could muster while still attending to all of his tasks at hand, "WITH GOD AS MY WITNESS, LEAVE THIS ROOM AND NEVER SPEAK OF THIS EVER, NOT TO ME, NOT TO MONSIGNOR, NOT TO THE BISHOP OR ANYONE…"

"To my dismay Deacon Eric, in the most cowardly and shrunken way, slithered himself back out of the sacristy as silently as he had come in.

"Going against all my will power, wishing, and praying to a god that obviously does not exist, Father J masturbated me to ejaculation. Upon witnessing this shoot from my penis, Father J could no longer contain himself as he also climaxed, putting his semen deep within my body and soul.

"The pedophile did not move for a brief moment as he relished in his ecstasy. He was sweating and panting as he pulled himself out of me and simultaneously reached for a white linen cloth embroidered with a gold cross on the corner. The cloth was folded ever so perfectly on the table. He started cleaning himself off, speaking softly out loud, but not speaking to anyone in particular: 'Lord wash away my iniquity and cleanse me of my sins,' were the words dribbling from his mouth, after which he threw the dirty, bloodied cloth at me. 'Clean yourself up boy! Hopefully you have learned your lesson and will fly straight from now on.'

"I am not quite sure how I long stood there in the depth of my despair, just staring up at that cross with my pants down and blood oozing from my backside. There were no more tears, just pure pain rushing through my soul, depleting me of any sense of hope or goodness in my eleven-year-old world. With the smoke of the incense still lingering, I did my best to stop the bleeding from my ass and shoulder as I tried to get myself together.

"I retreated from the sacristy, making the walk down the dingy hallway, through the silence of the vacant rectory, and back outside. I gingerly maneuvered my way down the six granite steps. My gait now had a limp due to the pummeling I had just barely endured. As I encountered the crosswalk to make my way back to school, I slowly took each step trying to manage the pain. There was no wind at my back and the stillness in the air was accompanied by a silence I have never experienced to this day. The carefree child that had traversed these same white lines earlier in the day, the one who had the conviction that anything, absolutely anything was possible, that child was pillaged of all his innocence and hope.

"Silently, I navigated my way through the last few hours of school. The final three o'clock bell sent me on my way, walking the now wet streets from the misting fall rain. I usually would be heading to the YMCA for swim practice, but I knew that was not going to happen. Even at the young age of eleven, I was a very accomplished and competitive swimmer. I had enjoyed the sport, but after that day's encounter, I would never again attend a swim practice. The darkness of the evening had fallen, and I found myself still slowly walking, drifting in and out of a walking consciousness. With a wet head of hair from the misting rain, I made my way to my house.

"As I lumbered under the old wooden train track trestle, the deafening roar of the cars bringing all the people back from the city rambled above me. The lingering thought of somehow making my way up to the tracks and laying my body along the steel raced through my head, knowing that the relief from my torture would be coming to me with the next passing train. But the physical effort to barely keep walking was an almost impossible task in itself. The deliberating thoughts fluttered away as the mental anguish overtook my brain again as I continued my journey home.

"Situated in the heights of my town, we lived in one of the wealthiest areas. My house was recognized as one of the most desirable houses on the hill. It had such a unique architecture. For one, it possessed more windows than any other house in the town. A good majority of them were stained-glass which made the dwelling a very sought-after house. The large, triangular one and half acre lot was extremely isolated. Setting solely on its own block, the dwelling had a street on each of its three sides, giving a great distance between our house and every neighboring house.

"As I entered the house, I heard the loud volume from the TV coming from the large den in which my father would watch sports. The den was encompassed with dark wooden antique furniture which complimented the similarly designed walls. Leather couches and large chairs were placed throughout the large room. There was a dark table next to each sitting area to support one's drink or cigar.

"As my father slowly sipped his gin from a short expensive crystal glass, he quickly took his eyes off the TV to see my wet hair. 'Oh good, you are home from swim practice. How was it?' he almost inaudibly asked as he immediately directed his attention back to the TV.

"Barely able to speak, for I had not vocalized a word since the funeral, I asked 'Dad, can I talk to you?'…no response…'Dad it is really important. Can I talk to you? Something happened…DAD,' I said with a little louder voice. My dad quickly interrupted me, without taking his eyes off the television. He loudly stated, leaving no room for misinterpretation, 'Can't you see that Game One of the World Series is on?'"

Thirteen

As the days bleed into early December, the team's anxiousness about not having apprehended Tiberius is mounting. They know that every passing day is a time of preparation and planning for Tiberius, bringing him that much closer to his next kill. They feel as though they are either making progress towards catching their guy or their guy is making progress towards his next victorious kill. They don't think Tiberius is going to wait much longer. His unbridled impulse cannot be contained. His inclination to kill is like a herd of wild horses running through the mountain ranges that just cannot be corralled.

The timeline of events is laid out on the four whiteboards in front of the team. There's a fifth new whiteboard off to the side, completely dedicated to Tristan Colburn and what Christine learned from her interview with him. The faces of the dead stare brutally back at the detectives. There is a yearning in their eyes, as if they are pleading with them to catch their killer.

As Gary is pondering the previous conversation with Tiberius, he finds himself almost conflicted. A very brief and faint memory from his days as young altar boy flashes through his mind, fleetingly causing him to question this one strange encounter he had with a priest.

He has never felt any sympathy for a suspect before. But after hearing the unfounded sexual abuse that was inflicted on Tiberius, he is finding it very difficult not to have at least an ounce of sympathy for the boy in the story. Gary knows he must be a professional. He must not have sympathy for Tiberius. He must not allow it to cloud his judgment, for the next victim's life is at stake. Gary has no room to be sympathetic and needs to keep his senses sharp.

Jake lays out what they know about Tiberius. "Okay, from our three conversations with Tiberius, this is what we have put together. We are looking for a white male in his thirties, with an outside chance of him being in his early forties. He is very intelligent. He has exceptional knowledge of computers, data manipulation, and internet configurations. He is a physically strong specimen. Most likely he lifts weights either at a gym or has a gym set up in his residence. He is someone that is capable of moving the one hundred-fifty to two hundred-pound victims around at will. He has very light, sky-blue eyes.

"He was raised, at least for a time, in a Catholic school. The school was associated with a Catholic church located right across the street. This church is where Tiberius served as an altar boy. We need to look for towns that have a Catholic school located directly across from the church. The church rectory has six granite stairs leading to the entrance. It is a large church, most likely having numerous granite stairs making the grand entrance to the front of this church. Like most Catholic churches, it is going to be older. The rectory has long dark corridors weaving throughout the maze-like hallways used to traverse one's way around. It is or was furnished with antique wooden furniture and has one fairly large metallic cross hanging on the wall.

"The town we are looking for has a YMCA with a pool. The YMCA is within walking distance of the school and church. The backdrop of his story depicts a very wealthy and well to do upbringing. A town that has large houses and good schools, possibly located somewhere in the northern part of a state, county, or town.

"We know that he was abused by a priest referred to as Father J. We know this priest had some type of possible nerve damage in his hand which caused his index finger and thumb to remain straight without the ability to curl like a regular finger. We do not know if this Father J is still alive or not.

"We know that the victim Father Eric O'Leary was previously killed prior to us finding him at our stake out. We know that Father O'Leary spent time in the same parish as this Father J. He was a deacon at the time and was a full-fledged eyewitness to the abuse of Tiberius, thus inducing Tiberius' fierce revenge that was inflicted upon him resulting in a most barbaric and heinous death. We are still yet to find the historical records of where Father Eric served his deaconship, only his various stops as a priest.

"As much as this is about revenge, as much as this is about making a statement and proving something, it has equally become a game for Tiberius to play against us. He has been a recluse most of his life and is probably for once enjoying the interaction he is having with us, in particular with Gary.

"We need to keep pulling on all these threads. Sooner or later we will find our way in, but we must be vigilant. From here, everyone go meticulously back over all our evidence. Tiberius has left an opening for us somewhere. I am convinced we will find a lead to go on!"

Fourteen

After a few hours of sleep, the early morning finds Christine sitting at her desk. It is with fresh eyes that she is staring at five photos from a decade-old killing. The autopsy report is missing from the file. But there is just something she cannot piece together. She has come back to this particular file and these pictures multiple times during her review of the many cold cases.

The killing took place ten years earlier on a playground of an elementary school, the Willard School in the town of Ridgewood, New Jersey. Ridgewood is one of the most northern towns in New Jersey. This link is one of the reasons why Christine kept coming back to this file.

The crime scene was discovered in the wee hours of the morning when the sky was still dark. The few streetlights, in the background, illuminated the eeriness of the pictures.

The victim was hung from the top center of an extra-large dome playground climber, a very common fixture on most school grounds, except this one was about three times the size of the average dome. The victim was found dangling from the waist down. He was securely tied with nylon rope at the waist, legs, and feet, leaving just his torso suspended in the air coming down through the highest opening in the dome. His mouth was duct taped shut. His left arm was tied twenty feet away to that side of the dome and his upper chest area was tied off twenty feet to the complete opposite side of the dome, leaving his right arm dangling, pointing straight down towards the ground.

The pictures showed the streetlight shining directly in the background of the victim. It made an uncanny resemblance to that of a darkened upside-down cross, as if the cross was being highlighted from behind with the light shining around its edges. The victim was stabbed in the neck and left to bleed out. The trickling of blood pooled in the sand in the center of the dome directly below him.

As she has been studying the photos for a while, she had requested them to be blown up for better definition, clarity, and exposure. Looking through a magnifying glass, Christine notices it for the first time. She realizes that the right hand is configured in such a way that the index finger is pointing straight down, and the thumb is pointing to the left while the pinky, ring, and middle finger are curled up towards the palm. Stumbling about her desk, shuffling through the paperwork, the frantic noises alert Jake and Ryan at their desks. She finds the paper she was looking for. It has the victim's name. Jean Hymebrick.

"Jean Hymebrick. That's it!"

"That's what?" Jakes inquires.

"Jean. Jean. Jean!" Christine repeats to herself standing on her feet holding the photo and the death certificate. "Father J.

This has a similar M.O. Duct tape covering the mouth. One arm hanging downward for the blood to drip from the hand. A puncture wound to the neck. Although he was tied with a rope and not duct tape, this has to be him. This victim has to be Father J! Father Jean Hymebrick. I know it! It has to be him; it has been misleading because for some reason the occupation of this victim was not filled out on the death certificate. This has to be Father J!"

Jake reaches for his phone and calls the Bishop at the archdiocese of Newark to get confirmation on this victim Jean Hymebrick having ever served as a Catholic priest.

"He has! Can you tell me what parishes he has served in?" asks Jake, repeating the answers out loud so Christine can write them down. "Prior to his death, he served at the Sacred Heart of Jesus in Mahwah, New Jersey, for the last twenty years of his life. Before that, he spent twelve years at Mt. Saint Mary's Church in Ridgewood, New Jersey. And his first three years of service were at the Holy Trinity Catholic Church in Cherry Hill, New Jersey.

"So, those are all the historic records you have on Father Jean Hymebrick?" says Jake, shaking his head in an up and down movement. "Yes, Bishop, it certainly was a brutal killing."

"Do you think you have found the culprit in his killing?" the Bishop inquires. "Is this cold case connected to the World Series killing or the Paterson killings?"

"We cannot comment on that right now, Bishop. I can say that this information is extremely helpful. It most certainly should help us continue our investigation. We will be in touch if we need anything else. Thank you again."

Gary was already researching the three towns while Jake was still on the phone.

"Cherry Hill is a very affluent town, but it does not have a YMCA within 30 miles. Both Ridgewood and Mahwah have YMCA with pools. I want Christine and Ryan to head up to Mahwah and check out the Sacred Heart of Jesus Church. Jake and I will drive up to Ridgewood and see what we can find there."

Fifteen

It is a bitter cold early December day. Snow is forecast for later this evening. The chill brings about goosebumps, raising Christine's brownish forearm hairs as she waits next to Ryan outside of the rectory. Ryan looks around as he pushes his hands deep down in his coat pockets trying to keep his warmth.

"I don't know, Christine. This isn't lining up. Here we are at the door of the rectory, adjacent to a small street, but there are no steps leading up to the door. Tiberius mentioned six steps leading up to the rectory entrance in his story. There are no steps here." Turning around, Ryan glances across the street. "Look, there are two small town mini convenience markets across the street which are surrounded by modest housing. No school or a building that a Catholic school could have resided in." Ryan takes notice of the architecture on the houses and the store fronts. "These buildings have been here for probably eighty to a hundred years."

As an elderly priest finally starts to open the door to greet them, Christine says, "Should we just head down to Ridgewood and catch up with Gary and Jake?"

"No. We're here. Let's ask some questions and take a look around."

"Hello, good morning, Father. This is Agent Christine Breeze and I am Agent Ryan Anderson. May we come in and ask you a few questions?"

"Yes. By all means."

Closing the door behind them, the two detectives find some much-needed relief in the overly heated foyer as they shake off the cold.

"Father, were you here when Father Jean Hymebrick was serving?"

"Yes. I was here. God rest his soul. That was a tragic ending to his life. That was unimaginable to me and the other two priests who resided here. Who would want to murder Jean? Especially so brutally!"

"Did you have any knowledge of Father Jean abusing any children? Physically, mentally, or sexually?"

"Heavens no. Not that I am aware of. He was here for a long time. I never heard of anything like that. To my knowledge no one ever came forward accusing Jean of that. He was a godly priest."

"Can you show us your rectory?"

"Yes, of course. Anything to help."

Making their way down a very short, well-lit hallway, the three enter a very small rectory. This entrance is the only door to the small room. The room contains some shelving and two small tables. Looking around, Christine shakes her head side to side, indicating that this is not the rectory where the abuse of Tiberius took place.

"Father, do you have a record of all the altar boys that have served here over the years?"

"Yes. I can get that for you. It was my department to oversee the few altar boys we had year in and year out. Not having a Catholic school to affiliate ourselves with, we did not have the opportunity to draw many young boys to help us serve. Let me print you those records. I have been here for thirty-five years. I probably have the last thirty years on record."

"That would be great. Thank you."

* * *

"Gary, this is Christine. I don't think Tiberius was from Mahwah. Things here do not match up to his story. We are getting a printout of the altar boys from the last thirty years. We're going to do some snooping around town and check out a few names on this list, focusing on those altar boys that would be in their thirties now. We'll see if we get any hits."

"Okay, Christine. Sounds good. We're almost to Ridgewood. Let's touch base later."

Jake takes the next exit off Route Seventeen, following the signs for Ridgewood. They drive through the picturesque, tree-lined streets that were established over one hundred and twenty-five years ago. The architecture of the stores and houses is what gives the area its small-town charm, an authentic, sought after charm that has failed to be replicated time and again across the country. It is the type of charm that cannot be manufactured or duplicated in this day and age. It makes for a very attractive location to the many affluent New York City business workers. Having only a twenty-mile commute with trains running in and out of the city multiple times a day only enhances the small-town popularity.

Passing a park-like town center decorated for the holidays, they pull up in front of the rather large Mt. Saint Mary's Church. The twenty granite stairs leading up to the three large double wooden doors for the main entrance make quite the statement. The magnificent, sand-colored stones used to build the church are highlighted with grand stained-glass windows. The enormity of the church is impressive. The two detectives notice the overall footprint of the building is that of a very large cross. The building is laid out on a three-acre lot that is solely occupied by the church and its self-contained rectory.

Driving past the front of the church, they take a right hand turn down the side street. They easily park on the vacant street that is directly outside of the rectory entrance. Hustling to keep warm, Jake and Gary jog up the six granite steps to the door and ring the doorbell.

Taking note of the six steps in his mind, Gary also turns to look at the building across the street which is constructed with the same stone colored bricks at the Church. He notices the Windsor Bergen Academy signage out front.

A middle-aged priest answers the door.

"Hello, can I help you?"

"Yes, we called earlier. This is detective Jake Blevins and I am detective Gary Hurst. We wanted to ask you some questions."

"Yes, yes, come on in."

As they traverse the doorway, Gary asks, "How long has the Windsor Bergen Academy been around?"

"About twelve years now. Not too long in the grand scheme of time. For a long while before that, it was our Catholic school as well as the convent. The convent housed the nuns that taught at the school. I do not know if you two are aware or follow the Catholic church, but we do not have the following we once had.

"Ridgewood has such great public-school options to choose from. This is why many families move to our town and pay the high taxes. We could not keep our school running with only five or ten people in a grade. That is what our attendance was down to. It just does not work out. So, we had to close the Mt. Saint Mary's Catholic School. Thankfully, we still have many devoted Catholic families that attend our church. Being situated in a very affluent town also helps keep our church more than solvent.

"You mentioned on the phone that you would like to take a look around the church and the rectory."

"Yes. Let's start with the rectory if we could."

Eeriness sets in as the priest leads them down two long, dark and very drab hallways and brings them to the rectory. Looking to his left, Gary taps Jake's arm to get his attention. They notice the long wooden antique cabinets situated along that whole side of the wall. Gary thinks to himself *this must be it.* He stares directly cattycorner across the room to the double doors which exit to the outside. The two doors have a large wooden centerpiece that the doors close upon.

Standing near what must be at least a hundred-year-old antique cabinet, Gary starts to envision the tragic abuse that was inflicted upon Tiberius in that very spot. Jake is sliding all the smaller drawers in the cabinet in and out, looking on both sides of each one. "Hey, Gary, look at this," he exclaims, showing the penciled numbers that are hidden on an inside panel of the wooden drawer.

Having not moved for a few minutes as he takes it all in, Gary says, "Yes. This is the place." His eyes are fixated on a barely faint outline of a cross that obviously hung for many years above the center of the cabinets, leaving an indelible mark.

He looks over at the priest for an explanation.

"An old metallic cross used to hang there. It hung there for probably eighty or a hundred years, leaving its mark that seemingly won't go away. It was stolen about ten to fifteen years ago. It was just never replaced."

With an inquisitive look taking over Gary's face, he asks the priest if he could get a ruler. "Yes, there should be one in the office down the hall." The priest returns a few minutes later with a ruler in hand.

Gary turns to Jake. "Hop up there and measure that outline."

"Will do, boss. What are you getting at?"

"Just measure it."

"It is twenty-one inches long."

"What about just from the cross bar down to where the bottom of the cross would be?"

Jake maneuvers his hands to get the measurement. "That's just twelve inches."

"Twelve inches. That is the exact size of the murder weapon we are searching for! Tiberius came back and stole the cross. That's what he is using to inflict his pain and kill his victims."

* * *

Meandering around the large marble altar of the main church, Gary and Jake look up at the oversized gold replica of the crucifixion hanging right above the center table. They wait for the priest to come back with the list of altar boys from the past. Astonished by the architectural beauty of this church, they walk past the long wooden pews which are uniquely engraved with a cross at the end of each one. Gary finds himself in deep reflection and takes a knee on the padded kneeler in front of the one hundred or so candles set off to the side of the main altar as one of the multiple prayer stations in this church. He brings his hands together as he points his fingers to the heavens. He rests his brow on his index and middle fingers as he settles into his prayer routine.

Dear God, please help us stop Tiberius before he kills his next victim. Give me the strength to be smarter than him. The strength to be one step ahead of him. Our father, who art in heaven, hallowed be thy name, thy will be done on earth as it is in heaven, give us this day our daily bread and forgive us our trespasses, as we forgive those that trespass against us…

Looking up at the cross in front of him, Gary grabs for a wooden stick and lights one of the many candles set in the dark red or blue glass which are set out before him.

Walking towards the doors, they pass the four confessionals embedded in the wall under the enormous stained-glass window which encompasses most of the south wall. Pushing through the big wooden doors, they are met by the priest holding a list of the altar boys for the last thirty years.

"Here are the names and address of the altar boys we have on record. At least the address at the time of when they served."

"Thank you, Father. This has been very helpful."

"God bless and God speed in catching this killer."

The two detectives walk out into the brisk cold air and Jake heads right to the door of the car. He turns to see Gary paused fifteen feet in front of the car, standing and looking down at the worn white lines of the cross walk. With his hands in his coat trying to defend against the cold, he cannot help but think about the eleven-year old boy whose innocence was stolen because he crossed the threshold of this simple crosswalk. Peering up the street one way, and down towards the silence beyond their car at which Jake is standing, Gary's heart can't help but feel some sympathy for the boy, wishing that those tragic events had never happened to Tiberius. Tiberius' life would have been saved and completely different, but also all of Tiberius' victims would still be alive right now. Even if they were pedophiles and abusive priests, it would be for the legal system to decide their fate and deal out due punishment.

The cold chill blowing down Gary's neck snaps him out of his thoughts and back into the task at hand. He wipes his wet eyes and turns to walk towards Jake.

Settling back into their car, rubbing their hands together for warmth as they wait for the heater to kick in, Jake calls Christine. "Hey, Christine, we want you to head down to Ridgewood. This is definitely where Tiberius was assaulted. We are sending you half of the list of the altar boys that served at Mt. Saint Mary's Church. We are going door to door to see if we can find this guy."

"Okay. Sounds good. We will head down to Ridgewood and start on our half of the list."

* * *

As they make their way house to house, Gary and Jake are not having much luck. At five of the houses no one was even home. Three of the homes had rather elderly occupants that were more than gracious to answer questions and some even offered some hot cocoa to warm their chill. Enduring the long stories at each of the houses about their son's success' and accomplishments, they were still not hearing anything that would connect them to Tiberius. After an hour and half of being polite and listening to one of the moms go on and relentlessly doting on her son, they realized that this particular subject had passed in college from a drunk driving accident. It was time to politely move on.

Darkness has fallen early on the December afternoon. Finding a parking space outside of Ridgewood Coffee at the center of town, Gary declares, "I need some caffeine before we hit the next few homes. Text Christine and tell them to meet us here as we regroup."

"Got it, will do."

Jake is settled at a wooden booth looking out the window at all the wealthy people of the town. They are hustling outside from store to store getting their holiday shopping underway. As the snow majestically falls on the town, Jake takes notice

156

of a particular mom. This happy go lucky holiday mom stops to unwrap a candy cane to give to her bundled up daughter who is cuddled up, laying back in the stroller. She has on her reindeer winter hat that is helping to keep her warm. Breaking away for a moment from the reality of their dire situation with Tiberius, this vision gives Jake a much-needed feeling of comfort. Seeing the kids and parents enjoying the holidays as the flurries of white snow are dusting the sidewalks and streets is just what Jake needs to continue with their quest.

Jake is almost halfway through his coffee when he checks his phone. "Still no response from Christine. They must be inside one of the houses conducting an interview."

"Let's give her a bit longer to finish up. Then we'll give her a call."

"Okay."

Becoming anxious as he finishes his coffee, Jake picks up his phone and calls Christine. Five rings later it goes straight to voicemail. "I will call the station to get their last twenty-twenty."

"350 Heightsman Road. Let's go catch up with them."

* * *

The early dustings of the anticipated snow have increased in volume and the town is now blanketed with about two inches worth. Christmas holiday lights beam from the large houses as Jake and Gary drive through the picturesque neighborhood. Catching a glimpse of a small wooden sign almost hidden in the nine-foot hedges surrounding the three sides of this uniquely isolated house, they turn right on Heightsman Road and pull up right behind Christine and Ryan's car. This particular house has no holiday lighting or decorations. It only has very dim lighting coming sporadically from some of the one-hundred plus windows that make up this old house. The car in front of them is cold and covered with snow from front to back, indicating that it has been sitting there for a while, at least since before the snow started falling a few hours ago.

Quietly getting out of their car, Jake and Gary close their doors without a sound. Unsnapping their guns but keeping them holstered, they make their way along the tall hedges to the opening at the driveway.

Jake looks at Gary. In an almost inaudible voice, he says "There are no footprints in the snow anywhere. If they are in there, they have been there a while. There are no signs of bright lights or any indication that a group of people are meeting inside."

"You go around one way and I'll go the other. We'll meet at the front door."

With guns now drawn, the two detectives separate as footprints mark their way in the snow. The two disappear from each other into the darkness of the night which is only lit by the rising moon's reflection across the snow on the yard.

Walking along the bushes next to the house, Jake peers into each passing window, not seeing anything at all. A light crunching of the soft unpacked snow indicates each step Jake takes as he canvasses the house. With his heart racing, he suddenly does not hear the snow crunching under his soles. He looks down to see a redness in the wet, almost melted snow.

Jake's eyes quickly follow the darkness embedded in the bright white, freshly fallen snow. He gasps as he sees Ryan's dead, open eyes staring him in the face from underneath the bushes. Ryan's neck has gaping holes on each side from which the warm blood escaped and melted the snow. The body is still warm despite the two hours that have passed since his neck was pierced right through. Ryan's death is at the hands of Tiberius, who drove the cross completely through him from side to side.

Jake quickly grabs his gun with both hands and brings it up in front of his chest. With his forearm, he wipes the sweat from his brow as he gets his breathing under control. Still making his way along the house, he finally comes across a side door. It is unlocked. He enters the dark house, squeaking his way through the kitchen as his wet shoes traverse the tiles. His way is only lit by a candle here and there. He immediately recognizes the music playing from a far-off distant room as the same Pink Floyd album that played in the background of their conversation with Tiberius. He glimpses a partially opened door down a hallway and cautiously heads in that direction. The squeaking from his shoes finally ceases as he now has a small hallway runner rug underneath his feet.

He notices there are only a few windows in the fireplace lit room as he cautiously makes his way around the slightly opened door. As he steps on to the now wood floor, his vision takes in the full view of what lies in front of him.

Sprawled backwards over the leather couch, Christine is naked. Her ankles and wrists are chained to the floor as her legs are spread wide apart facing the fireplace. The whiteness of her skin reflects the shadows of the dancing fire. Her seemingly soft, fluffy, neatly shaped, pubic hair sits at the pinnacle of her arched body. The pubic hair is book ended with her dense hip bones on each side which are protruding up towards the ceiling. The flatness of her belly shows the indentation of her navel.

In her upside-down position, the gravity is pulling her skin taught, showing the strength of her rib cage. As her shoulders press against the front panel of the couch, the firmness of her white breasts lay in all their glory, with her perfectly shaped, soft nipples drawing near her face. The paleness of her cleanly shaved underarms leads to her strong fit arms. As her arms outstretch across the dark stained wooden floor, her blue veins stream themselves down to the metallic bonds holding her hostage. Her palms face the ceiling with open hands, and her arms are pinned against the floor. As the top of her shoulders find a resting place on the floor, Christine's head is slightly tilted to the left side. Her blue eyes are dazed, almost closed, as the drool slides off the side of her almost oversized lips. Her hair was taken down from her usual professional bun to be strewn elegantly, without effort, across the floor. The beauty of Christine is laid out gracefully in the center of the room as her strapped down body has an unmistakable resemblance to a cross.

"Christine! Christine!" Jake says trying to get her attention, but not too loud to alert Tiberius, for he does not know where the killer lurks. He beckons again. "Christine!"

There is only a moan barely given in response. The opioid-induced haze that is rushing through the veins of Christine is still in full effect.

Jakes takes a full step closer to help Christine.

With the quickness of a cold winter breeze rushing across the ice of a frozen lake, Tiberius steps out of the darkness and slides a needle full of heroin into Jake's carotid artery. Jake is helpless as his body slides to the floor. Tiberius grabs the gun from his hand. Retrieving the handcuffs from Jake's waist, he secures him to the mooring that holds the chains attached to Christine's left ankle. Fishing Jake's phone out of his pocket, Tiberius throws it towards the fire.

Admiring the two detectives that he has subdued in front of him, the warmth of the fire glows against Tiberius' high cheek bones. He hears a creak from the hallway outside the room and makes a break for the door on the opposite side of the room.

With his gun drawn, Gary enters. He sees the back of the killer fleeing the room as he quickly unloads a shot. Barely missing his right shoulder, the slug implants itself in the wooden door frame. He kneels to the floor to take Jake's vitals first because he is closest. Finding a pulse, he rushes to Christine's side. Relief cascades through his body as he realizes they are both just heavily sedated.

"Hang tight, I am going to get Tiberius," he quietly tells the two detectives. With all the speed that his sixty-plus year-old body can muster he bolts for the door that Tiberius just made his exit through. Christine is left helplessly moaning in front of the fire.

Hearing the sound of running feet crossing the house, Gary does his best to make up ground. Exiting a long hallway, he dodges the long wooden dining room table, and passes the three antique pictures on the wall which are only illuminated by the candles on the side tables. The scattering of noises coming from the second floor brings Gary to a winding stairway in the far corner off the house.

With the sounds of the Pink Floyd album overtaking the house, Gary's eyes could not be wider as he slowly checks the second-floor hallway. His gun drawn straight in front of him, he clears the corners and his blind spots as he methodically moves forward. Noticing light coming from underneath one of the bedroom doors, he presses his ear up against it, only to hear a slight hum, a sound that could only come from something mechanical. This light is different than all the other lighting in the house. All the light up to this point has been from a candle or the fireplace. This light was coming from something else.

Turning the handle slowly as the door creaks itself open, he quickly pops his head around the door, then pulls it back. Once again, he does a quick check and pulls his head to safety. Moving around the door, Gary sees what is producing this light. The blue and green shades of light are coming from six large computer screens all mounted on the wall above a very large wooden desk. The manmade hum is coming from the computers situated next to the desk as the machines seems to be working feverishly trying to find the solution to some problem. He clears the corners and steps back into the hallway.

Something drops to the ground down the hallway by the stairs and Gary starts running towards the sound. Tiberius is already at the bottom bolting his way through the first floor. Following the loud footsteps, Gary hears a side door swing open and shut again. Making his way down to the first floor, running at full speed, without missing a beat, in full pursuit of their killer, he opens the door and runs out into the night.

His first step hits the ice on top of the porch, sending both of his feet flying into the air, bringing him crashing down on his backside. The back of Gary's head is first to take the impact of the fall, cracking his head open and leaving him unconscious as the stars and the moon shine down through the frigid December night.

Having just swung the door open, only making it sound like he left the house, Tiberius slipped back into the pantry, hiding in the shadows as the detective flew by him and cut the door.

The door slowly opens, and Tiberius makes his way out to stand over the detective. Kicking Gary's gun out into the yard, he reaches for the detective's two sets of cuffs. He affixes each arm outstretched to the bottom of the steel railings on each side of the porch. He leaves Gary's head and shoulders where they hit the cement. His torso and legs are laid out down the six stairs making their way to the ground.

Tiberius places the thick, right bottom sole of his Doc Martens across the side of Gary's neck. Rolling it back and forth, he halfheartedly tries to revive him back to consciousness. He stands tall at the top of the steps towering over Gary's cross-shaped body splayed down the stairs in front of him. He lets the coolness of the air brush across his face as he basks in the light of the moon.

The otherwise quietness of the night is pierced by the gentle melodic guitar intro bellowing from the dark recesses of the house. The eeriness of the bass line bridges the lyrics to life.

"Hey you! out there in the cold, getting lonely, getting old, can you feel me?... don't help them to bury the lie(ght)."

The song "Hey You" by Pink Floyd settles Tiberius' emotions as he patiently waits for Gary to come around.

Coughing and gasping for a bit of air, Gary slowly lifts his heavy eyelids to catch his first glimpse of Tiberius towering over him. Tiberius' breath is painting clouds into the bitter coldness of the night. The light of the moon shrouds the outline of his face. Gary sees his chiseled chin and protruding brow, his piercing, sky blue eyes, and his more than shoulder length, thick, black hair. The veins on his hand and forearm glisten in the light of the moon as they bulge from the tight grip he has on the cross he uses as his murder weapon. The blood-stained cross-sword is readied at his side, as if he was a warrior in battle.

"It is a pleasure to finally meet you face to face, Gary. Tell me, how is your day going?"

Coming out of his daze, Gary realizes his unfortunate dilemma. "Not too good right now. Things are not really working in my favor." He winces at the pain coming from his head.

"What's the matter, Gary? Didn't you pray today? Didn't you ask God to take care of you today? You have to admit, Gary, I might be on to something here. This whole prayer and God thing you so highly admire might not be its all cracked up to be. It reminds me of a time when I was young. Younger than when I was an altar boy, even. Every Sunday my Mom and Dad would take me to church.

"There was about this two-month period that I kept noticing one of my classmate's fathers praying at the little prayer station off to the side of the altar. It was on that side of the church that all the confessionals were housed. Anyway, it left a unique impression on my memory. Mr. Hopkins would kneel and pray in front of these dark red and blue glass candles. It was during the colder months, kind of like it is now. I remember that because he was always heavily clothed, usually wearing a scarf. He had gold, wire-rimmed glasses and he did not have any hair anymore, although, he used to. He had these three metallic posts that were set into his head near each of his temples.

"It was after every Sunday mass service that his family would go outside and he would remain and pray. He did this, like I said, for a few months. Then I did not notice him anymore. I do remember his daughter Angela who was in my class being very upset because her dad had died. I figured he had some sort of brain cancer. The metal posts in his head were guides for the radiation treatment he was enduring every week.

"I ponder that he was praying to God to help him get better. He prayed a lot. He probably prayed a lot more than just when I saw him. So, any sensible person would venture to guess, after all that effort and praying, that his prayers would be answered. Well … maybe not so much. He still died, leaving his daughter, son, and wife behind."

Putting two and two together, Gary realizes Tiberius is referencing the same praying station that he knelt and prayed at only hours before.

"Tiberius, you have to be more open minded than that! It is all about perspective. How do you know if Mr. Hopkins' prayers were answered or not? Maybe they were."

"I doubt it," bellows Tiberius.

Gary sees an opening to try and persuade Tiberius.

"Try to think about it this way. Prayer doesn't necessarily change the will of God. Prayer doesn't change God's attitude towards me. It mainly changes my attitude towards God. Praying helps us to know and to try and understand God's will for us. Prayer helps us to have acceptance of God's will in our lives."

"So, please tell me, Gary. Was it God's will for Father J to be fucking me in the ass? Was I supposed to be accepting of his penis shoved deep inside of me? I just should have prayed over the situation! Sometimes you disgust me, Gary."

"I know you are in so much pain. Please, let's just put an end to all this. I understand what happened to you, Tiberius. We can help you. Things are different than they were thirty years ago. We can help make you better. We can get justice for you against all the pedophile priests. We can make it right.

"God gave us the greatest gifts in the world. He gave us intelligence. He gave us the ability to choose and decipher right from wrong. I believe all is right with God's world. He gave the world different spectrums to experience. He gave us the ability to feel happy, the ability to feel deep sadness, and everything in between.

"God gave us free will, which is almost the greatest of all gifts I might say. The ability to do with as we will with the opportunities put in front us. The ability to have perspective in this life. The ability to be grateful or the ability to squander every gift or opportunity laid before us. He gave us that. His son sacrificed his life so the rest of us could have this.

"Just do the next right thing. You know what the next right thing is. I know you do. I know you have goodness within you, Tiberius. Everyone does. You can walk in the sunlight of the spirit! Doesn't that sound good? Put all this chaos behind you. No more running. No more hiding. You do not have to kill anymore."

"I am walking in the sunlight of the spirit, as you would say, Gary. I am doing for the world that which nobody else would. I am being of greater service, per se, to your god, than anyone else. I am ridding this earth of the vilest of men, the lowest form of dirt that might possibly exist in mankind. I am taking that task upon myself to destroy them, to bring them to justice for the horrible wrongs that have been inflicted upon the innocent. No one else had the decency or courage to bring these disgusting perverts to righteousness and give them what they deserve. I am doing the right thing. I have the fortitude to protect the innocence of children.

"I will agree with you then. I guess this is my free will to do what I want. It is my free will to clean up this world and rob these most repugnant people of their lives. Not unlike what they so freely stole from me at the young age of eleven. Those so-called priests used their own free will to prey on children and to destroy their lives. I think I might like your logic on all this free will topic after all.

"You see the moon shining down upon us now? I believe in the moon, the stars, the sun, and the ocean. You can always count on them. No matter what, the stars and the sun are going to shine. No matter what, the moon is going to reflect the light of the sun down upon us even during the darkest of nights. No matter what, the ocean's tides will always come and go, just like clockwork. I can unequivocally count on those things to happen. The moon, the stars, the sun, and the ocean, they will never let me down.

"You don't even have to pray for it, Gary. It is just going to happen. Those are the things I believe in. You see I do believe. I believe in self-preservation. I believe in survival. Hell, I was taught that at a very young age.

"You know, as far as poor Ryan goes, that was just unfortunate. He just got caught up in my self-preservation. He almost had me with the element of surprise. But as usual, I gained the upper hand. Sorry, it just had to be done.

"Do you think Ryan was praying for God's will as this steel cross pierced his neck? Do you think Ryan was praying for acceptance as his blood oozed out into the snow bringing him to his demise? Do you think his prayers helped him have a better attitude towards God as he has now left this earth, no longer to be with his child or partner?

"It just doesn't seem to me like God was shedding any grace on Ryan tonight. What do you think? Is he shining any grace on you right now? Or is that just the moon shining down upon you?

"Now for Christine. She is someone really special. Earlier in the evening, I had the pleasure of standing near her. I just stood there, smelling her pussy. It was delightful. It was so incredibly unique. Like no one's I had ever had the gratification of encountering before. It made me really look forward to my time with her later.

Brushing the hair back from his face, he asks, "Have you

ever smelled her pussy? C'mon, be honest now. You must have at least thought about that sweet young thing at some point?"

"No. I never have."

"Never have what?" Tiberius asks as he places his foot back on Gary's neck and starts pressing down hard.

"No, I never have smelled her pussy."

Tiberius smirks with a half-smile. "I figured as much. I just really like making you say it though. You see Gary, you are in quite the quandary. You are so desperately trying to stop me. With valiant effort, I might add. But I don't you think you realize that trying to stop me is like trying to stop the cold elegant wind in the dead of the night that is blowing intently across a snow-laden prairie. It is already headed in that direction, it has a course that it must take, and it is not going to be diverted. Yes, that is what you are up against.

"Gary, the world needs people like me. The world needs me. The world needs me for the never-ending debate of whether God is, or God is not. They need me to prove what flimsy beliefs they might have.

"The atheists need me because having someone like me helps support their disbelief in God. Certainly, if there were a god, this god would not allow a man like me, with so much evil lurking around in his soul, to be let out on the loose.

"As for people of religion, such as Catholics and other Christians, they need me desperately. Because when someone like me comes along to avenge all the sickness their leaders have unrightfully inflicted on the innocent, they think they need some sort of god to pray to that will somehow make them feel better. To have some mythical belief that their prayers will make the evilness go away. They want to be able to just turn it over to God. To have something else take the responsibility for all the wickedness in the world. To relinquish them from their part in it. Thinking that praying will allow them to just wash their hands of the situation and turn a blind eye because some so-called god will take care of it.

"That is one of the differences I have learned. I just took the responsibility upon myself. I did not need some fake god or non-responsive god, or some god that was never going to save me or never going to show up for me. False hope was continually delivered to me over and over again by the church. But when I was in my most desperate time of need, there was no god. There was nothing. Just me getting raped up my ass at the hands of a priest, bringing me to the most incomprehensible demoralization ever conceivable. Your so-called God just let me endure it at the hands of one of his so-called leaders of faith! But still, you all need me. You all need me to justify it. One way or the other.

Struggling to pull at the cuffs attached to the railings, Gary is at a loss for words.

"I bet you are even silently praying right now. Praying for your life. Am I right?"

Gary shakes his head in agreement.

The pool of blood thickens around Gary's head. The darkness of the sky is only being interrupted by the stars and the fullness of the bright moon, for the peaceful white snow has stopped falling. The faint sound of the music playing in the background and the sound of Tiberius' breath painting the air can be heard in the otherwise silent night. In the far distance, the sound of sirens begins to wail. Tiberius looks upward as he hears the sirens breaking through the cold, dark night.

With Tiberius pressing the pointy metallic end of the cross deep into Gary's neck, but withstanding the desire to pierce the skin, he states with conviction "It seems that our short time together has come to an end, Gary. Too short at that. For as always, I was really enjoying our conversation. Maybe your prayers were answered after all. Because it seems I must acquiesce and leave you alive and all too well.

"I now must ask a favor of you before I depart. For I need you to tell Christine that I cannot wait to meet up with her again. I will cherish the smell of her pussy in my mind until I have it with me again. Tell her it will be something to look forward to.

"As for you, Gary, don't you worry. We will certainly meet up again as well. I am quite sure of it."

Tiberius releases the pressure from the cross pressing into Gary's neck. A sense of solace starts to draw Gary in and out of consciousness. Gary is fighting to stay coherent as the moon lights the way for Tiberius to make his way down the stairs to the yard. Gary vaguely hears Tiberius' large Doc Martens crunch the snow as he trudges his way to the driveway. The old wooden garage door creaks upon opening and the brown van's engine begins to rumble. Gary has no choice but to stare up at the stars that are so eloquently displayed in the beauty of the midnight blue sky. His breath slices the cold-crisp air as the fading sound of the van is lost in the streets, for Tiberius has vanished into the safety of night.

Koi Shif draws constant inspiration from Tom Clancy's late success in life and JK Rowling's desperately humbling beginnings as an author. With JK writing her early, yet unknown stories, within the cafés of England, as her young daughter slept beside her, with barely enough to get by, is strength enough to live by. Having been rejected by multiple publishers and for the fact that they both persisted until they found a pathway for their success to unfold is brilliantly courageous.

Koi believes that uncertainty is a virtue. He believes that adversity is primed to be over come and that stories should be shared and written about. He believes in the dichotomy of agony and success through life. He believes that darkness is fleeting, as it too shall be lightened, for the sun will once again shine down upon us.

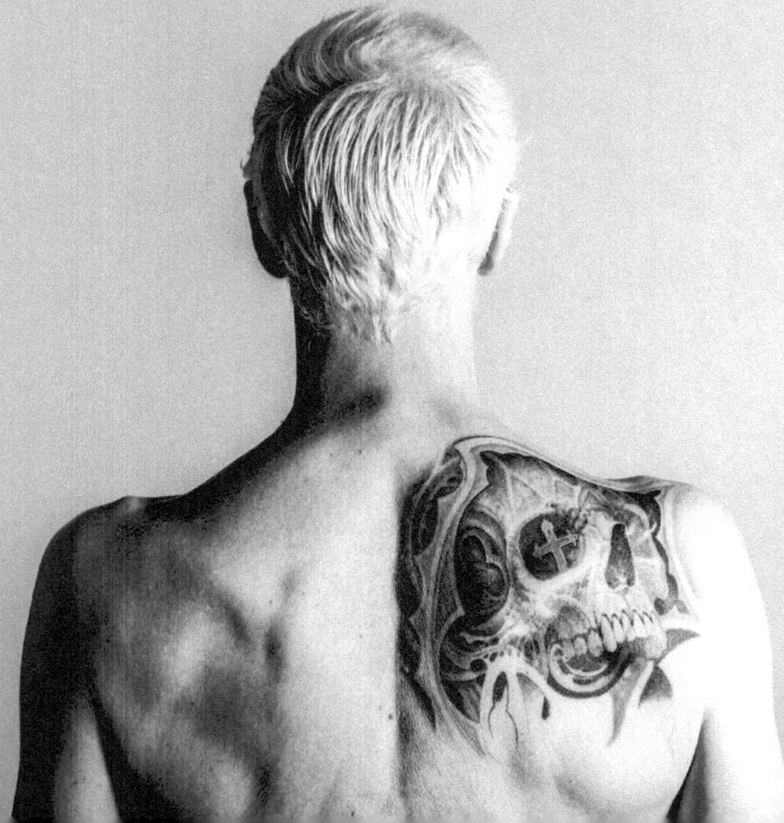

www.ingramcontent.com/pod-product-compliance
Lightning Source LLC
Chambersburg PA
CBHW050408190726
48284CB00007BB/2482